THE *Dirty Heroes* COLLECTION

BOUND *in* SACRIFICE

INTERNATIONAL BESTSELLING AUTHOR
MURPHY WALLACE

The Dirty Heroes Collection

Once upon a time, a scorned Queen opened
a box, unleashing horrible evil on the world's
heroes.

Instead of gallantry and chivalry, they now
possessed much more perverse traits. They've
fallen victim to their darkest and most deviant
desires.

This is one of their stories...

BLURB

Bound in Sacrifice

A regular at my club racked up a large debt that he couldn't afford, so I sent my men to collect. Instead of delivering the money I was owed, they brought me her. Unable to fulfill her father's debt, I told her he would pay for it with his life. When she begged to trade her father's life for her own, I was intrigued. But she couldn't hide the shiver of fear cloaked beneath the façade of strength and bravery she tried to portray.

Silly girl, you don't know what you've gotten yourself into. I'm going to snuff out your pride and stomp on your courage.

My father was a good man with strong values, who put his family above everything else. We weren't perfect, but we were happy. Then, Mom died and took our happiness with her. Dad quickly got caught in a downward spiral that spun our world into chaos. The warm, caring man that I knew from my childhood was replaced with a complete stranger.

It sucked the light from my world. Now, I fear I will pay greatly for his transgressions.

GLOSSARY

Bound in Sacrifice

La Tour - The Tower - France's most exclusive BDSM club

Le Côté Débutant - A side of La Tour meant for people who are new to BDSM or who are casually involved in the lifestyle.

Le Côté Avancé - A side of La Tour meant for people who are fully immersed in the BDSM lifestyle.

Le Couloir - The back half of La Tour. It contains playrooms and dungeons for a couple or group to act out a scene.

Moniteurs de Dungeon - Dungeon Monitors - Employed by The Beast; they ensure the safety of the members.

Esclave de maison - House Slave - someone who performs household duties, much like a maid would do, but they are generally in a state of undress.

Le Château - The Beast's Castle

CHAPTER ONE

The Beast

THE CLUB IS CROWDED TONIGHT, BUT THEN again, our open houses always are. Everyone wants a glimpse of what goes on inside of La Tour. It's the country's most exclusive BDSM club, and everyone who's anyone comes here to play, whether they're open about their propensity for kink or not.

Of course, there's a lot more to be desired when our non-members are here. We want to tease them; to work them up, and then turn them away. It drives them mad in all the right ways. Inevitably, they end up begging us to take their money just so they can see more, so they can scratch their itch. Once they get a taste, they never want to leave.

They're only allowed on Le Côté Débutant. Things are more relaxed over there since it's filled with people who are here for a good time, and people who want the chance to try different things, meet new people, or possibly connect with a new Dom or sub. It's where our beginners go to learn, but sometimes it's more like New Orleans in the middle of Mardi Gras; a fucking shit-show.

No one is allowed on Le Côté Avancé until they pass our specialized course. That side is solely for our advanced members, people who have been in the lifestyle for a while, respect the rules, and know how to behave. It also tends to be where our wealthier members opt to play, and we like to give them a sense of privilege while they're here.

There are two sides to the club for a very specific reason. I've seen my fair share of idiots who think that it's okay to walk into a scene and start participating, simply because they're at a BDSM club. They think that everyone who is here is ready and willing to be touched.

Wrong!

Tonight, I'm perched high above the action

on the catwalk that runs over the entire 7000 sq. ft. club. There are two main play areas, as well as Le Couloir, which is where you go to access the dungeons, the playrooms, and the backstage area. From up here, I can get to any area of the club I wish without ever needing to look at or speak to anyone. Other than my office, this is the only place in La Tour that I can stand to be anymore.

This used to be my happy place. It used to be everything in the world to me. But, no matter how badly you fight for them to stay the same, things always change. My feelings splintered into a thousand pieces several years ago, when Viv was ruthlessly taken from me.

But I refuse to think about her anymore.

I'm torn from my thoughts by the sight of a peculiar girl moving through the crowd. Her plain hair and clothing are stark in contrast to her astounding beauty. Between that and the air of innocence surrounding her, she sticks out like a sore thumb.

Who *is* she?

I've never seen her in here before and she sure as shit doesn't look like she belongs here.

The other women filling the floor are clothed in scantily clad dresses or donning barely-there lingerie, while this outsider is draped in more clothing than 10 of the other women, combined.

How did she make it past reception dressed like that?

I stalk her from my perch like a bird looking for its supper. She looks worried and irritated as she furiously searches the area around the bar for something or someone. The nipples on her ample tits are barely hidden behind the thin button-up shirt she's wearing and the demure bra, that I'd bet any amount of money she has on.

Is she here with a date? Is she meeting someone? Why does she look like someone just kicked her puppy? She turns toward the bar and leans over it, trying to get the bartender's attention. The swell of her ass looks like it's just big enough to fit in the palm of my hand.

What's most puzzling though, is why I'm thinking about her the way that I am. Why am I so interested in this strange woman? I haven't shown this much interest in any girl since Viv. It's probably because she's so out of place here.

Someone who isn't cut out for a place like this is a threat to my business and all of the members. I need to keep a close eye on her. We don't need any problems, especially during an open house.

She finally gets the bartender's attention and they exchange a few words. She turns from the bar, looking exasperated, and searches the room once again. As if she can feel me staring at her, she looks up. Her eyes widen in alarm when they lock onto mine.

What's wrong, little lamb? Can you see the beast inside of me?

We stare at one another for longer than I'd care to admit. What is it about her? I don't look at females like this anymore, and I certainly don't waste my time on them any longer. But there's something about this female, which draws me in. The fire in her stare burns bright, but not bright enough to hide the scared little girl that she has locked away within her. Not taking my eyes from her, I begin to walk toward the ladder that will lead me down to the floor of Le Côté Débutant, to where she is. I break eye contact for a split second as I turn and place my boot on the top rung of the ladder and begin my descent. I shouldn't have taken my eyes from her, because by the time my feet hit the floor, she's gone.

"Master Vilé," one of the members greets me and nods when I pass him. I nod in return. I think. I meant to, but right now I am on a mission and can't worry about that.

I scan the room. She won't be at the bar because she just left that area. I gaze out over the guests on the dance floor. It's so thick with bodies that I can't tell where some people end and others begin. There's no way she could've squeezed her way through there so quickly.

Come out, come out wherever you are. I need to find you. I need to know why you're here.

I scour the outer edge of the room, where all of the play areas are located. I highly doubt I will find her participating in a scene, but could she be a voyeur?

Finally, my eyes land on her at the back of the room, pushing the door to Le Couloir open.

That's a big no-no, little lamb. No one allowed in Le Couloir on open house nights. The corner of my mouth turns up in a sly grin as I think about everything that I could do to her back there.

Walking briskly, I follow her path to the back of the club and open the door leading into Le Couloir. I expect to see her when I open the door, but no one is there. There are two corridors in this hallway and I choose to go left. I stalk down the darkened passage as quietly as I can, so I will be able to hear any noise that she might make if she's come this way. I carefully wiggle the doorknobs on each of the playroom doors as I pass by. They're all locked, as they should be, so I know she hasn't run inside one of them to hide.

"Father?" I hear suddenly, echoing from the other end of the hall.

I stop and turn on my heel at the sound of her angelic voice.

Father?

Is she playing some sort of Daddy Dom/little girl game? I pick up my pace so I can catch up to where she is before she can get away again. When I get to the center of the hallway, where the two corridors meet, I sense that she's near. I flatten my body against the wall and wait for her to arrive.

Just as she steps away, I materialize from around the shadowed corner. She gasps in surprise and tries to hide her fear as she realizes she's been caught somewhere she shouldn't be.

"What do you think you're doing back here?"

"I'm--I'm sorry. I'm looking for my father. When he leaves and doesn't come back for hours, this is usually where he comes," she stammers but then she swallows her fear, letting a burst of confidence shine through.

"Your *Daddy* comes to Le Couloir?" I ask her, knowing that's not at all what she meant, but I'm aching to see her blush.

"What?" she's honestly confused, missing the reference. "No, he comes to this disgusting, depraved, worthless pile of stone for desperate sex fiends and alcoholics!" She holds her arms out, regarding the club as she speaks, with bitterness flooding her tone.

"Disgusting. Depraved. *Worthless*? You talk about my club like you know something about it, little lamb."

I step forward slowly, and she backs up. I may not hold the same regard for La Tour that

I once did, but no one talks about my *home* like that.

"*Your* club? So, you're the reason for this abomination?"

I hasten my steps, backing her up into the wall behind her. My hand wraps tightly, but not dangerously so, around her thin neck and I force her to look up into my eyes.

"You think you're better than all of those people in that room over there?" I cock my head slightly toward the door leading to Le Côté Débutant. "That your morals and values mean more than theirs?"

Anger flashes in my stare, and I feel her shiver beneath my touch.

"Why do you think that? Who told you that you were better than anyone else? Your *Daddy*?"

Her fear deepens, judging by her widened doe eyes and increased heart rate, that I can feel beating rapidly beneath my palm. It matches the beat of my own dark heart. Does my touch affect you, like the feel of your flesh affects me, little lamb?

"You don't like it here because you don't belong here. We don't want you here. So, you're going to go back to the perfect little life that you fell out of and never set foot in this *disgusting, depraved, worthless pile of stone* ever again."

I bring my face dangerously close to hers, forcing her to see the evil within me, not allowing her to look away.

"The club isn't the abomination, *I am*. If you ever step foot in here again, you're going to find out exactly how far an angel can fall."

I release my grip on her neck before I lose complete control and throw her down into the dungeon. She scurries off through the door to Le Côté Débutant, and disappears into the crowd of members and guests.

I stand there, seething as the door closes, shutting me into the darkness where I prefer to be.

CHAPTER TWO

"**Y**OU HAVE TO EAT, FATHER," I URGE AS I place the plate of eggs and bacon on the table in front of him. With his eyes still closed from sleepiness, his hand searches for his fork.

I wasn't able to find Father at La Tour before that beast of a man ran me off the premises. He was right, I didn't belong there. If I never have to go back there it will be too soon; I am nothing like those people.

Because you're too chicken shit to do anything remotely exhilarating.

My inner voice is a nuisance, and it constantly reminds me how, at 23 years old, I'm still very much a child. I've only had one boyfriend, and while I am not a virgin, I wouldn't be considered an experienced lover. I want adventure, but I fear it will always be just out of reach, and I can't have a life of my own while I'm forced to be my father's keeper.

Seeing all of the people in the club last night, laid out, tied up, and put on display like they're a meal about to be eaten, it made me feel uneasy. It scared me, but it also intrigued me, although I am not entirely sure why.

Was it the lack of decency, of virtue? Baring everything to a room full of strangers? Or was it the fear of the unknown that leaves me unsettled? I would be lying if I said that I wasn't the slightest bit curious to find out more about that type of lifestyle. But, not after having had my run-in with that brute.

Do you mean the one who caused the ache inside of you to bloom with desire? The one who drove you to consider touching yourself last night? You would have if you weren't consumed with worry over your father.

I chide myself for thinking like that and cast the thought from my mind. I'd sooner marry Gavin and have the rest of my life planned out for me than think about the monster for one more second. Gavin is my slime ball of an ex and he's awful in nearly every way, but at least he's no savage.

Father finally came stumbling up our driveway around 3:00 this morning. He mumbled something about Reggie and then passed out on the sofa. I don't know what to do about him anymore. He is my father and I'll never give up on him, but I can't, *we* can't keep living like this. We're up to our eyeballs in debt because of his drinking and that awful club. I don't know how he can even still afford to pay for his membership. He hasn't worked in over a year and his unemployment money is long gone.

"Father," I speak up once I realize he's fallen back to sleep. "Father!"

I jolt him awake with my words and force a cup of coffee into his hands.

"Drink up. You have a job interview this afternoon."

He grumbles his annoyance and takes the mug of hot liquid from my hands.

"Rosabelle," he speaks up after several

mouthfuls of coffee, "Whatever happened to that promotion that you were supposed to get at work? We would be fine living on just that salary alone."

"Father," I pause, trying to compose myself, but the anger is boiling within me. "You should already know what happened with the promotion," I manage to get the words out through gritted teeth.

A few weeks ago, I got a call in the middle of the day to come and pick up my father from Philippe's, a bar in the city that my ex-boyfriend's family owns. My father was drunk... again. As much as it pained me to do so, I begged Gavin to keep an eye on him for me, just until my interview was over. Gavin thinks he's God's gift to women, but he's nothing more than a disgusting pig. He said he would watch father, but only if I promised to go out to dinner with him. I agreed, just to get him off of the phone.

Imagine my surprise when, in the middle of the interview, my boss, my supervisor, and I heard shouting coming from the office lobby of our office. We left the conference room to find the source of the commotion and found Gavin hitting on the receptionist. My extremely drunk father had tripped over one of the chair legs, fallen to the ground, and was unable to get up.

I'd never been so mortified in my entire life. When I was finally able to get Gavin out of there and put my father in a cab for home, I was able to explain the situation to my boss. I told him how my mother died three years ago, and my once perfect father had fallen into a deep depression. With Mother gone, I took over the duties she left behind. Father and I made the most out of our situation for a little while, but he was never the same. Once my knight in shining armor, the man who I looked up to and loved most of all, became my greatest burden. My boss said that she understood and that I would be allowed to keep my job, but she wouldn't be able to promote me at that time.

Fucking Gavin.

I should have just asked my boss if we could reschedule the interview. I *knew* asking Gavin for anything was a mistake. When we were together, all he would talk about was getting married, and having me quit my job so I could stay home and take care of the brood of children he wanted to have. *No, thank you*. I want much more out of life than to stay at home and be a kept woman, and especially not *his* kept woman. Taking care of my father these past few years has taught me that this is not the life that I am destined to lead; at least, I hope it's not.

After the incident at my office, Gavin told me that his offer of marriage still stood and that I wouldn't have to worry about anything ever again. He promised that he would take care of Father and me, and money would cease to be an issue.

If I wasn't so angry at him that day, I might have taken him up on the offer. Even in our small, modest house outside of the city, we can barely afford to live on my salary alone.

"Why don't you just accept Gavin's offer of marriage, then? It would make our lives so much easier."

"No, Father. It would make *your* life easier," I feel myself cracking beneath the surface. "I'm not going to marry someone just so you don't have to work, or have to worry about where your next drink or fuck will be coming from."

The shock of what I just said to my father hits

both of us at the same time. I've never spoken to him like that before. The hurt in his eyes is palpable and guilt settles into my stomach like a boulder.

"I took impeccable care of this family for 25 years! Is it too much to ask that someone take care of me in return, Rosabelle?"

He throws his fork down on the table as he rises out of his chair. He shoots daggers at me as he rushes out of the kitchen, and down the hallway to his room. I hear the shower turn on and I hang my head. I know I shouldn't have spoken to him that way, but I've had enough. I didn't mean to be disrespectful, but it's been a long time since *I* got any respect around here either.

That needs to change. Starting today.

I watch the seconds tick away until I get to go home. It has already been a very long and tiring day and I don't know how I'm going to make it until 5:00. Between my late night and the fight with my father this morning, I'm surprised

I've made it this long without crashing. I've contemplated asking to leave early several times, but can't bring myself to do it. I rarely take leave, and the disastrous events that occurred a few weeks ago are still fresh in my mind. I don't want to press my luck by asking for a favor so soon. I don't know if I'll ever be able to rid the stain on my reputation that day left behind. Just as I've talked myself into getting back to work, my office phone rings.

"Provincial Marketing, Rosabelle speaking," I recite into the receiver.

"Hello Rosabelle, this is Mr. Roberts from the bookstore."

"Mr. Roberts, hello," I respond, hoping he's calling me to say he's hired Father.

"I've been expecting your father for his interview, but he hasn't shown up yet. Are you with him? Do you know if he's still coming?"

Fuck.

I can feel the hot, angry tears forming in my eyes. My father blew off his interview. After this morning, I don't know why I even assumed he would still go freely.

"I'm so sorry." I can't stop the tears from

THE DIRTY HEROES COLLECTION

falling this time. "I'm not with him. I should have known this would happen... Please, forgive me for wasting your time, Mr. Roberts."

"Rosabelle, you know you're not wasting anyone's time. Whenever you can get your father here for the interview, whether that's today, tomorrow, or next week, I'm okay with that."

"Than--thank you, Mr. Roberts. That means a lot to me," I hiccup as I wipe tears from my face.

"Come on in, anytime. Try to enjoy the rest of your day, then. Goodbye."

Mr. Roberts is an old friend of my mother's. I reached out to him last week asking if he had any positions open for hire. I know my father can't hold down a decent, good-paying job any longer, so I'm not even going to try it. I thought that he'd at least be willing to give this place a try. All he would have to do is put books away, and ring people up at the cash register.

I quickly shut down my computer and gather my things. Looks like I *will* be taking the rest of the day off. I have a good feeling that I know where my father is and he is *not* going to be happy to see me when I get there.

CHAPTER THREE
The Beast

I WASN'T ABLE TO SLEEP MUCH LAST NIGHT, which is nothing new, but this time was different. I couldn't get the scent of that girl out of my nose, or her exquisite beauty, especially with my hand at her throat, out of my mind. I told her to never step foot in here again, and I meant it, but the darkness that rules my life prays she disobeys. As hard as I tried, I couldn't keep myself from picturing her tied to the bondage bench in my personal dungeon.

I close my eyes, thinking back to the imaginary scene I whacked off to last night. Her back was to the leather, arms and legs spread wide, with her tits and her pussy on full display just for me. I basked in her beauty. With my dick in one hand and my crop in the other, I circled her. Tapping her clit, her tits, her nipples with the crop. No part of her was safe from me, from the torment. Then, I turned her over and painted her pale ass a rosy pink color with my flogger...

"Yo, Beast."

I am pulled from my trance by Dex, a senior member of my security team. He nods his head toward the crowd below when I glance in his direction. Following his gaze, my eyes lock on a regular named Mauro, who has been known to cause trouble from time to time.

"How the fuck did he get over there?" I ask, rhetorically, wondering why he was allowed to set foot on Le Côté Avancé.

I dart across the catwalk toward the ladder closest to that section, never taking my eyes off of him. I've had the fucking shits of this guy. He's a drunk, he's rude, and he's disrespectful to the girls. I should have kicked his ass to the curb a long time ago, but Reggie, my business manager, vouched for him so I've given Mauro a little leeway as a professional courtesy to Reggie. No more though; I've fucking had it.

"Luca!" I shout to the closest man I have on

the floor.

His gaze, as well as the gaze of several members, shoots up to me from his place next to the bar.

"Get him!" I shout, pointing at the dumb fuck.

Mauro's about to encroach on a scene at the spanking bench. Just as he reaches his hand forward, ready to run it over the girl's ass, the guy rears back and punches him square in the jaw. I'm glad he did it because now it means that I don't have to.

Luca runs over and stops the fight before it can get out of hand. I jump down from halfway up the ladder and stomp over to the spanking bench.

"Take this piece of shit to my office and wait there for me."

Luca removes the drunk idiot from the floor and disappears with him into Le Couloir.

"Master Shaw, my apologies for the intrusion. Is your sub alright?"

"She's fine, but I expect a hell of a lot better here, Vilé. We pay too much money to have to experience this kind of issue."

"I don't disagree. Come see me the next time you're in, and we can work something out," I speak quietly and extend my hand to him. He shakes it and nods his acceptance of my offer.

"Nothing more to see, folks," I shout, letting everyone know that the show is over. "If you go to the bar, Cohen will give everyone their next round on the house."

Cohen, a head Dom and one of my best friends, moves from the floor to the bar area and readies himself for the onslaught of people at the mention of a free drink. The chatter in the room rises up once more as mingling continues and scenes resume. I assess the crowd once more, ensuring everyone appears content. When I am satisfied that all is back to normal, I hurry into Le Couloir, which will lead me to my office. I stop just inside the door and my eyes fly to the spot where I had my little lamb pressed against the wall last night. My dick grows hard and the corner of my mouth twitches with the hint of an evil grin. I may have to bring up the security footage from last night once I've finished tending to business.

When I get to my office, Mauro is in the chair in front of my desk, and blood is dripping from the corner of his mouth. He's lucky. If it were my scene that he interrupted, he wouldn't be breathing right now. Luca is standing behind him to make sure he can't run away until I say so. I settle into my seat and cock my top lip into a sneer at the sight of the filth in front of me.

"Who the fuck do you think you are, imagining that you could ever belong on Le Côté Avancé?"

"Oh, fuck off with your rules and thinking that you're better than everyone else." The words fly from Mauro's swollen mouth just before he spits a mixture of blood and saliva on the floor next to him.

Big fucking mistake.

Before I have a chance to jump over my desk and knock his ass out, Luca has him out of his chair and rips the shirt from his body. He balls the fabric up and throws it at Mauro's feet.

"Get down on your hands and knees and clean it up, *now*!"

The motherfucker doesn't move and Luca

sweeps his feet out from underneath of him. In one swift motion Mauro hits the floor with a thud, knocking the wind out of him. Fucker. I'd like to knock more out of him than just that.

Luca picks up Mauro's shirt from the floor and throws it in his face.

"Fucking clean up your mess, before we make an even bigger one by tearing your body from limb to limb!"

I have to hide the snicker that threatens to escape. The funniest part about this is how nice and genuine Luca usually is. He isn't even my muscle, that's Cohen's role. Luca looks up at me and I can't help the grin that spreads across my face. He shrugs his shoulders at me and smiles goofily. Then, his slightly embellished look of outrage resurfaces on his face as he looks back down at our guest.

I hear some shuffling around on the ground and take it that Mauro has complied.

"Good, now get back up here, sit down, and keep your fucking mouth shut," Luca points to the chair and in seconds I am forced to look at Mauro's ugly mug again. As kooky as Luca is, he's a damn fine Dom and knows how to assert his authority.

"Mauro, you've been a member here for how long now?"

"Two years," he answers, disgruntledly.

"Okay, so *more* than enough time for you to know the fucking rules, then."

I pull up his account on my computer and review it.

In the past two years, he's been forcibly removed from the club seven times for different reasons. Jesus... *seven times*? I really have had my fucking head up my ass, haven't I? How the fuck did I not realize this?

I keep looking through his file and I see something that doesn't make sense to me. There are transactions listed, but every single one of them has been comped; discounted to nothing. Thousands of lines of transactions over the past two years, but not one penny paid. From bar tabs to playroom rentals. One thing I don't see on this list is his monthly membership fees.

I begin to see red.

What the *fuck*? Looking closer, I notice that every single comp was approved by my business manager, Reggie. I knew that they were close, but I didn't know that Reggie was *robbing* me blind! I wonder how many other members he's been letting in here for free?

I pick up the desk phone receiver and tap the extension to the bar where Cohen is.

"Hey, get someone to cover the bar. I need you in my office."

A few minutes later I hear a knock at my door.

"Come in!" I shout. "Cohen, hey, I need you and Luca to escort Mauro downstairs. He's going to be staying the night."

"What? Downstairs?!" Mauro shouts. "You can't do that! It's kidnapping!"

"Let's go, fucker," Cohen commands.

Him and Luca each grab one of Mauro's large, beefy arms and pull him in the direction of my office door. It's not easy due to Mauro's size, but he's had enough to drink that he can't fight them off easily.

As they walk into Le Couloir, I wonder what other shit Reggie may have been pulling these past few years. I look through the books some more and notice that a fraction of all sales, membership fees and otherwise, is being funneled into a different account.

What the fuck?

I pick my phone up again and reach out to one of our original members. He works for the Bureau of Taxation and we've done a few favors for one another over the years.

"Master Mayhew, I'm sorry to bother you at this late hour, but I'm afraid I've just come across a very large, extremely dire financial issue. I could really use your expertise as I work through it. Are you able to come in tonight? I'll waive next month's fee for the inconvenience in addition to whatever I owe you for the work. Excellent, thank you so much. See you soon."

I place the receiver back in its cradle, then lift it again, phoning the reception area to let them know that I am expecting Mayhew, and to escort him to my office as soon as he arrives.

If he confirms that I am seeing what I think I'm seeing, then heads will roll.

CHAPTER FOUR
The Beast

WHAT MAYHEW FOUND IN MY BOOKS LAST night has rocked me to my core. I thought I had an issue when Mauro interrupted that scene, but that's nothing compared to what my real problem is.

I knew that Reggie would be in today, so I opted not to call him in last night and cause him to panic. I've been waiting rather impatiently for him to arrive. The second that I see him walk through the doors, everything in me wants to punch his fucking face in. Thank God Luca and Cohen are next to me when he approaches, otherwise, I would do just that.

"Hey guys, how's it going?"

I nod and grunt in response.

"You haven't seen Mauro around yet, have you? His daughter has been blowing up my phone all day. She said that he never came home last night."

Mauro has a daughter? I picture him in a dress, and my face contorts in disgust.

"Haven't seen him since last night," I say.

At least that's the truth.

"Okay, thanks," he answers.

I let Reggie get settled into his normal routine and I try to go about my day, business as usual.

Around 11:30 that evening, I call the reception area. One of the house slaves answers and I ask her to find Reggie and send him to my office.

I have Luca and Cohen waiting for him in Le Couloir. They'll escort him to the dungeon where I'll be handling my questioning.

Thirty minutes later, I am on my way to one of my private dungeons to meet Luca, Cohen, Mauro, and Reggie. This particular dungeon is situated one level down from La Tour. None of the members and hardly any of my staff know that it exists. Luca and Cohen do because, through all of the shit that's happened, they've always been there for me. After everything went down with Viv, they were the ones who helped me pick up the pieces.

They're both Doms here and they each specialize in their own type of kink. Luca prefers wax play. The way he paints his partners with it is pure art. He's meticulous and knows exactly where to drip the hot liquid to increase sensation. Cohen, on the other hand, he loves his machines. He has distinct originality about him. I don't know anyone else who can pull off the steampunk look as well as he does, but his signature top hat and monocle look sure does entice the ladies.

When they aren't engaging in a scene with their own subs, they're in charge of the Moniteurs de Dungeon, in addition to guiding other Doms and subs through our instructional program.

When I reach the dungeon, I see Luca has already brought Mauro in and cuffed him to a chain attached to the far wall. He's sitting on the ground looking bored. He's despicable. He doesn't even look concerned for his *friend* across the room. Cohen mentioned a struggle, which would explain the swelling around Reggie's left eye and the blood pouring from his nose.

I walk over to Reggie and look down where he's sitting, chained to a wall on the opposite side of the room from Mauro. I squat down on my haunches and force him to look me in the eye.

"Reggie, I saw some very disappointing transactions when I was looking through our books, earlier. It *appears* as though you've been letting Mr. de Villeneuve partake in our club's activities for free. When I noticed that I did some more digging. Do you know what I found?"

He looks at me but doesn't say anything.

"Do you have anything to say to me?"

Nothing.

"So, you can lie to me, cheat me out of my money, but you don't have the balls to tell me why."

"I--it's not what it looks like."

I stand and try to reign in my temper, but

I can't. His lie infuriates me. How can it be anything other than what it looks like? I pick up my foot and swing my leg forward with as much power as I have, kicking him in his stomach. He grunts with pain and it only spurs me on more. I manage to get in two more kicks before I feel a hand on my shoulder. I turn my head in the direction that the hand came from and meet Luca's eyes. He's telling me to stop. To not make another mistake like I did as a result of losing Viv.

I turn my attention back to Reggie, who is laying in a heap on the stone floor of the dungeon, and then force myself to move away from him.

"Mauro, I spent last night adding up every last dime that you owe me. I suggest you think of the fastest way to get me my money or else the only way you're going to leave this dungeon is in a wooden box."

"It's not my fault that he never charged me for anything! You should be making him pay you the missing money."

"Oh, don't you worry about your pal Reggie over there, he's going to get what's coming to him."

"I--I don't have a dime to my name, there's no way I'll be able to pay you the money."

"Then I guess I'll have to find something else of yours to take as payment."

I pull out my cell phone and call Dex.

"It's me. Grab V and Andre. I need you guys to pay a visit to a member's house for me; Mauro de Villeneuve. He won't be home, so feel free to go in and grab anything of value, all of his most prized possessions. Bring whatever you find to me. This member owes the club a *huge* debt. He'll pay for it with his life if he has to."

Father didn't come home last night. I've been on the phone with Reggie several times today trying to find out where Father is, but he has no idea either. He said he hasn't seen him since the night before last when he dropped him off at home.

I went to Philippe's straight from work yesterday thinking that may be where he went instead of his job interview, but I didn't find him there. One of the bartenders said that he was there earlier in the day, but they kicked him out for starting a fight with other patrons. I was worried but figured he was off stewing somewhere, especially after the argument that we had, and would come home late as usual.

I tried staying awake to wait for him, but ended up falling asleep around 4:00 this morning. I ran to his room when I woke up, thinking he might have come home and I didn't hear him, but he wasn't there and his bed was undisturbed from the night before.

I called my boss to explain the situation and to let her know that I wouldn't be in today. Then, I contacted the police station to see if they had picked him up, but they didn't have a record of him being brought in. Same thing with the hospitals. As I felt my greatest fear coming to life, losing what's left of my family, I broke down. Eventually, I pulled myself together enough to realize there was still one person who could help me; my last resort.

Gavin.

"Rose, I'm glad you're here." Gavin pulls me in for an unwelcome hug when he sees me. "It makes me so happy that you'd come to me when you're in trouble, knowing that I'll be able to take care of you."

The feel of his hands on my body disgusts me and he knows that I *hate* being called Rose. His sense of humor and the good-natured personality that attracted me when I first met him two years ago is long gone. I think that I was blind to his ego and lies because of losing my mother. I was feeling vulnerable, and with my father no longer able to be there for me, I fell for the first guy who was. I lost my virginity to this snake, even though I wasn't ready to. He is the last person that I want to rely on, but I don't have any other options. Gavin knows this city and the people in it better than anyone else I know. Not that I have anyone else, anyway.

When I get to Philippe's, Gavin directs me to a booth in the bar so we can talk. Unfortunately, that means I have to be close to him, rather than out on the street with his crew, looking for Father.

"Gavin, stop," I say, pushing him away from me, "I'm really worried about Father. He's never been gone all night before."

"Rose, I have my guys out looking for him. I told them to bring him here when they find him. You don't need to worry about anything else right now, other than keeping me company."

I'm trusting that what he's saying is true. I called him and explained the situation before coming in. By the time I got here, supposedly, his men were already out looking. I need to believe him.

"I can't just sit here and not do anything about it."

"I can think of something we can do." his eyes gloss over with desire and his unconcerned attitude turns deadly serious.

"Gavin, I am not going to have sex with you."

"Rose, this negative attitude you have about us has gone on long enough. What happened?" he asks, exasperated. "We were so good together."

He's getting annoyed and I'm beginning to get nervous. I never should have come here.

"No, we were *never* good together. You should know that since you were the one who did all the cheating."

"I never cheated on you, Rose. I love you! I always have."

He places his palm on my cheek and attempts to pull me in for a kiss. Placing my hands on his chest I do my best to shove him back, but it's like trying to move a brick wall. I duck my head out of the path of his incoming lips.

"No--stop, Gavin!" I scream at him, attracting the stares from several other patrons.

He scoots my body further back against the wall and forces his hand between my legs. I grab his wrist with both hands and twist. Thankfully, it has the desired effect and he groans in pain as he removes his hand from me. I can't climb over him, so I drop down to the floor and crawl under the table to get away from him.

"Gavin!" I shout once I am back on my feet, alerting anyone who isn't already staring at us to our argument. "You're so infuriating!!! Do you think it was easy for me to come here and beg you for your help? If you're trying to extract some kind of payment for helping me, then it's not worth it. If you can still find it in your heart to help me, then please give me a call if you find my father. If not, then--then--go to hell!"

I turn on my heel and walk from the bar. My lame insult falls in the space between us as I exit the building. I remind myself that I am a strong and independent woman. I don't need help from anyone, especially not from a snake like Gavin de Beaumont!

CHAPTER FIVE
Rosabelle

After leaving Philippe's, I walked around the city looking for Father. I ducked my head into every single bar that I could find, with no luck. After five hours of nothing, I finally gave up and decided to go home. My blisters have blisters and the muscles in my legs feel like jelly. I haven't had any updates from Gavin. Either they're not looking or they haven't found him. I don't know which would be better at this point. I pull into my driveway, hoping Father might have come back and will be there when I get inside. I am alarmed to see an unfamiliar black Cadillac Escalade in my driveway when I pull in. The front door to our house is wide open and, stupidly, I run as fast as I can into the house thinking maybe something awful has happened to Father.

When I get inside, I witness two large men standing in my thoroughly ransacked living room. They incite terror in me with their sizable muscles and angry expressions. They don't see me right away and if I had any amount of sense in me, I would back away, run from the house, and go straight to the police station. I blame my behavior and lack of initiative on stress and fatigue from spending five hours wandering the city.

"What are you doing in my house?" I shout at them like a fool.

Rosabelle! Get the fuck out of the house. Run away, you idiot!

The thugs turn at the sound of my shaky voice. My eyes go as wide as saucers and I tremble with more fear than I ever remember feeling before. It's then I notice the emblem on their tight black t-shirts...*La Tour.*

Father. Oh my God, what have you done now? Or, are they after me because of my altercation with that monster the other night?

"Mademoiselle de Villeneuve?" the one on

the left asks me.

"Y--yes?" I can barely get the word out and even when I do, I don't even hear myself speak.

They prowl toward me and I turn to run. Before I can go anywhere, one of them hooks their arm around my neck. I faintly hear them tell me that they don't mean me any harm, but how can that be? They have me in a chokehold and I can see the darkness closing in on my vision.

The last thing I think before everything goes completely black is, I wonder if they've killed my father and if they're about to kill me. Then, to make myself feel even worse than I already do, I tell myself I don't care if I die, just as long as I get to see my mother again.

"I told you if I caught you inside of my club again that I would show you exactly how far an angel can fall."

The man's voice shocks me awake. I open my eyes only to find that I am tied to a cross like the one I saw when I was at La Tour *the other night. My ankles and wrists are bound to the posts, stretching my body out like a letter "X".*

"Yet here you are again, little lamb."

The monster from the club steps into the light so I can see him clearly.

He stands in front of me holding something that looks like the streamers which hung from the handlebars on my bike when I was a little girl. I am completely naked and laid out like a piece of meat for him. I'm ready for him. I want him.

I wait for the shock to come.

For the fear to tear me apart.

For the shame to hit me.

Why am I so calm? No, calm isn't the right word.

Content. I'm content lying here, being his.

His?

I'm anxiously awaiting his touch, awaiting the sensation of the leather tails across my skin.

None of this makes sense.

"My little lamb. My Rosabelle."

My name sounds lovely coming off of his lips...

"Rosabelle!"

When consciousness returns to me, I hear someone screaming my name.

"Rosabelle! Please no! She doesn't have

anything to do with this!"

Father.

My eyes fly open and I'm looking up into the shadowed faces of three huge, brawny men. They're standing around, staring down at me. My vision is still fuzzy and with the light shining above them, their faces are shrouded in darkness, making it impossible to recognize them. Frightened, I shoot up into a sitting position, quickly shuffling back, so I can get away from them. I immediately regret it when the headrush hits and I am almost sick.

One of the men squats on the ground and places his hand gently on my back, surprising me. His touch isn't hard or violent like I would have expected, but it doesn't mean anything, and it doesn't reassure me.

"*Don't* touch me!" I shout, squirming away from him and crawling across the cobblestone floor toward my father. "Father!"

"Rosabelle, oh, thank goodness you're alright!"

I kneel on the ground next to him and pull him in for a hug, while still paying attention to our surroundings. We're in an aged circular room that looks like it was built centuries ago. It's damp, musty, and humid. There are no windows on any of the walls. I desperately scan the room for the exit, for some way that I can get us out of here. My eyes land on Reggie, lying bloodied on the ground across the room. My gaze lingers on him for a moment before I turn my attention back to my father.

"I thought you were dead!" I say to him, "I didn't think I'd ever see you again!"

Tears begin falling from my eyes and onto my cheeks before I even realize that I am crying.

"Well, this is touching," I hear a familiar voice sound off behind me and my teary eyes grow wide with fear.

The monster from the club.

Turning toward the origin of the voice I see his face clearly now, and he looks even more sinister than he did the first time we met.

The events of the past few days come back to me.

La Tour.

Father's disappearance.

The men at my house.

No.

"What's happening?" I whisper, looking back into my father's eyes.

I can tell that he is as scared as I am, but he doesn't speak. He has no explanation, and no reassurance to offer me. Why would I have thought any differently, simply because our situation has now turned dire? Why did I expect him to snap out of the childish, destructive, irresponsible state that he's been in for the past two years?

"Tell me, little lamb, are you a thief like your father?"

No, Father. Please tell me this isn't true.

"I'm no thief and neither is my father!" I shout, turning my attention to the beast who accosted me in his club two nights ago.

I rake my eyes over the monster's enormous form; everything about him screams intimidation. His dark hair is cut short and his eyes are as black as night. I look into them, trying to see what he's hiding beneath his deadly stare, but it's too much; he's too intense and I have to look away.

Not only do I fear him, but my body is responding to him in a way that I simply don't understand; I want him. But, how can that be? I cast the thought from my mind and reason with myself that I'm terrified and confused.

Tattooed skin covers his muscled arms, and as I scan his substantial hands, I remember how he wrapped them around my throat the other night. They look like they could crush a coconut without any resistance. He has blood on his knuckles and I immediately glance back at Reggie.

That explains all the blood.

"Mauro, it seems your daughter doesn't know the first thing about you," the monster says. "Would you like to let her know why you're here or should I?"

I turn my attention to my father once again, leaning back so I can see him more clearly as I stare at him in confusion.

"Father? What's going on?" I ask him softly.

He continues looking between the monster and me. The longer he goes without speaking the more fearful I become.

"Father, what is he talking about?" I say more forcefully before whispering, "What have you done?"

"Rosabelle, I..." he begins but he stops there.

I try giving him a minute to pull himself together and tell me what it is he needs to say, but he can't do it. He hangs his head in shame.

"This is ridiculous. I'll fucking say what this good-for-nothing, piss-poor excuse of a man can't," the monster interrupts. "Your father has been stealing from me. Over the course of two years, he's racked up a bill of over $275,000."

I gasp at the total in utter disbelief. It's almost laughable!

"There's no way--that's not possible. There's been some kind of mistake!" I look from the monster, and back to my father. His head is still hung in shame and he doesn't even try to offer an excuse. Not even a lie to get him, to get *us* out of this situation. "Tell him, Father! Tell him that this is all a mistake!"

I bang on his chest at his lack of explanation. Even that doesn't emit a response from him. I feel my body go slack and let gravity pull me down to the ground beneath me. As I sit there in shock, the monster begins speaking again.

"Not one membership fee has been paid. He hasn't paid for any of the 10 events that he's attended, nor has he paid for one drop of the alcohol that he seems to drink as though it's water."

Still struck with panic at what is unfolding around me, I try to think clearly. Am I really shocked that Father has gotten himself into a situation like this? Well, a *little*. I suppose I've been waiting for something like this to happen, but I never expected it to be *this* substantial.

I thought maybe I'd have to bail him out of jail, a few hundred dollars, for being drunk and disorderly. I've been saving money from each paycheck, knowing I would need to use it for him. But $275-- I can't even think the number without feeling dizzy and sick again.

Taking several deep breaths, I try to clear my mind and steady my heart rate. I think about the money that I have in my account in addition to the little that I have stashed in my closet at-- *oh fuck*.

"Your men, did they find--" a lone tear runs down my face at the idea of strangers in my personal space. The idea that *he* was the one who sent them there.

"Your money?" the monster answers. "Yes,

THE DIRTY HEROES COLLECTION

they found that and they took anything else that they thought might be of value, which wasn't much."

He looks down at me with disgust and I can feel the rage blossoming within me.

"I *detest* you," I hiss at him. I've never been so angry at anyone in my entire life, except maybe my father. I want to punch him. I want to make him hurt as much as he's hurt me.

He crouches down in front of me, invading my space, and brings his face too close to mine. His smell assaults my senses. The delicious combination of citrus and spice is actually helping to soothe my anxiety and I hate the effect he's having on me. It fuels my rage and tears begin to pour down my face once more, making me angrier that he gets to witness me breaking.

He reaches out and grabs my chin firmly, but not hard enough to bruise. "The feeling is mutual, *little lamb*."

His eyes narrow as he rises back up to his full beastly height. "So, let's discuss payment options. Between the money and items from your house, you have about $5000 already. I think it's safe to assume that you don't have much in your bank account."

It wasn't a question and I am furious that he is correct. I notice he's only talking to me. Does he know that Father doesn't have anything to his name? Does he know that I am the only one with an active bank account?

"How much *do* you have?"

I stand and hold my head high, reminding myself that I am Rosabelle de Villeneuve. I am smart, strong, and independent, and I will never let anyone try to tell me otherwise.

"I'm sure that we can work this out between the two of us. A proper business deal? One that doesn't involve handcuffs, creepy dungeons, or violence. One that doesn't need to be discussed in front of a group of people whom it doesn't concern."

"I'm afraid that's not how this is going to work. This isn't a small, inconsequential business deal, as I'm sure you can understand. This is theft and, frankly, I should have already *dealt* with the issue. I don't need to give you an opportunity to make it right, yet here I am. Now, you're going to tell me how much money you currently have available to you, or I am going to show you exactly what I do to people who steal from me."

He pulls a handgun from his waistband and aims it at my father. I scream in terror, my hands flying to my mouth in fear.

I study his face, frantically searching for any sign that he might be exaggerating, but there is none. I don't think he would actually kill my father, but I can't chance it.

"No! Please! Please don't! I have approximately $30,000 in my savings account," I hold my hands out to him, begging him to put down the gun, and providing him with the answer that he wants.

"And what kind of job do you have?"

"I am an assistant at a marketing firm."

"So, no more than say, 40k a year, right? And that's being generous."

My eyes shift between the monster and his gun, which is still pointed at my father. I try with all my might not to be embarrassed that I make so little. I have nothing to feel ashamed for. I take care of my family and we have everything that we need to survive.

"Well?" he asks, waiting for my confirmation.

"Right."

He is such a pompous prick.

"The way I see it, little lamb, you're screwed."

"No, that's not true! I can give you the $30,000 immediately and I can make payments to you over time. It will take a little adjusting, but that should be sufficient. And Father, he has an interview coming up and then we will be able to--"

"No," he cuts me off.

"No? What do you mean, no? That's a perfectly good option if you--"

"I said, NOOO!!!" he roars.

I hurriedly back away from him in fright. He moves closer, placing his hands either side of my head, boxing me in. I hear the gun's metal thunk against the stone next to my ear.

"This isn't 'Let's Make a Deal'. This is hundreds of thousands of dollars, maliciously stolen from me. I say what goes and what goes is *Daddy.*"

"What? Wait!"

He turns back toward the center of the room

and addresses his men.

"Cohen, uncuff our drunken thief and take him out back."

CHAPTER SIX
The Beast

I GIVE MY KILL ORDER AND COHEN APPROACHES the worthless piece of shit. The second I turn away from the achingly beautiful girl in front of me, a shriek of terror tears through the air.

"No!" she screams, "ME! Take me instead! Please!"

I feel her soft, petite hand tug on my arm. Her touch is like fire on my skin and I turn to look into her eyes. Tears are falling heavily, rolling down over her cheeks. The sliver of make-up that she has on and doesn't need, is smudged, she's a beautiful mess.

I picture her on her knees at my feet. Only this time her tears are a result of my cock, lodged deeply in her throat.

My dick hardens in my pants as I imagine it.

What are the odds that a worthless idiot like Mauro would be the reason she entered my life? I stare into her beautiful hazel eyes, not wanting to look away. I couldn't even if I tried, she has completely enchanted me. I didn't know that I could still feel so strongly about a woman again.

The poor, helpless, sacrificial lamb that she is. She has no idea whose pasture she's wandered into.

Before I ruin everything by showing any kind of weakness, I remove her hand from my arm and eliminate the burn of desire.

"You silly, little girl, you don't know what you're saying."

"Please don't hurt him, he's all I have left in this world."

"Whether he's here or you are, you will still be apart. Would you really be willing to give your life for his? This selfish imbécile isn't even trying to talk you out of what you're offering."

She looks from me to her father and the tears fall faster.

See who he is, Rosabelle. Your life is priceless

compared to his, don't waste it on a man like him.

"If you do this, there's no taking it back. You will be mine...forever."

The thought of her being mine fills my body with lust. "I know," she concedes.

She breaks the connection with her father when she looks at me again, and I catch a hint of desire flicker in her gaze before her head droops with the weight of her grief.

"Take her down the hall while we get rid of our other problem."

Nodding to Luca, he walks over to her and gently takes her by the arm.

"Wait, please! Can I say goodbye first?"

I sneer between her and Mauro. He's hurt her this much, yet she still loves him.

"Make it quick."

Luca lets her go and she runs toward Mauro, throws her arms around him, and sobs. He doesn't deserve her. He didn't even try to stop her from giving herself to me in exchange for his life.

Fucking fool.

"Rosabelle, I'm so sorry for all of this! I will find a way to get you free from here! I promise!"

My anger grows at the thought of him freeing her from me. I nod my head to Luca and he grabs her softly, pulling her away from her father.

"I love you!"

She manages to get the words out before she's removed from the room. Her sobs echo behind her. I turn back toward Mauro and I want to knock his fucking face in for what he's done; not to me, but to her.

To Rosabelle.

The mere thought of her name lures a possessive growl from deep within me.

"Get up," I spit at him.

Slowly, he picks himself up off of the floor.

"You don't deserve her. You didn't even fight to save her from me. You're a worthless piece of shit and what just happened here is *more* than enough proof of that. You're never going to see your daughter again. Not that you will, but try not to lose any sleep over this. I'll take real good care of her."

"If you touch *one* hair on her head, I'll--" he begins.

I cut him off with a punch to the stomach.

His body folds on impact and his head lands on my shoulder. I speak into his ear, whispering so only he can hear me.

"Oh, I'm not just going to touch one of them, old man. I'm going to touch *all* of them."

I push him back and scowl, daring him to try and fight me. I would love nothing more than to take this motherfucker out.

"Cohen, take this worthless fuck out the back door of the club like the trash he is."

Cohen walks forward and unlocks the chain from the wall, leaving the cuff around Mauro's wrist. He tugs on the chain, walking him out of the dungeon and I am left alone with Reggie.

I turn and look at him. He's just as pathetic as Mauro. I close my eyes and shake my head. I'm exhausted, and I don't have the energy to draw this out.

"I don't have time or patience to enact my revenge on you the way that I would have liked."

He screams out, begging for someone to come help him, as I pin him down and encircle his neck with my arms.

"There's no one left to hear you scream," I

whisper sinisterly.

I squeeze him with all of my strength and firmly twist my arm, quickly snapping his neck and killing him instantly.

❧

Rosabelle

"Here you are," the blonde man who escorted me out of the dungeon waves his hand into the cell in front of us.

I want to ask him if he's joking or if I am *actually* to be relegated to living in a cell while I'm here. But the fact that none of what has happened tonight makes any sense keeps me from opening my mouth.

I enter the cell and he locks the door behind me. As I turn and face him, another man's terrified plea for help rings through the corridor and I gasp in fear.

"Father!"

"No, it wasn't your father," he says to me.

"What? How--how do you know for sure?" I sob.

"Because, The Beast always keeps his word," he answers. "He said he wasn't going to kill Mauro."

"Sorry if I am not reassured by that statement." I roll my eyes at him.

He turns, taking a step down the corridor, back in the direction from which we came.

"Wait! Please! Can you talk to him? Can you let him know that he can't just keep people locked up like this? If he wants to sue us, then by all means!"

"Sorry," he says, and for some reason, I actually believe he means it. "When The Beast has his mind made up, there's no talking him out of it."

The Beast.

I've been referring to him correctly these past two days; it's not hard to see why people call him that.

"It's a rather fitting nickname," I glower.

"You've got that right," he snorts. "Look, I shouldn't say anything, and if you tell anyone I did I'll deny it until the day I die, but you're not in danger here. I know it feels that way but The Beast, well, *sometimes* he's more bark than bite."

"*Sometimes*. That's just as reassuring as the last bit of information you gave me," I scoff.

"I'm Luca." he offers me his hand through the bars of my cell door.

He just locked me *in a cell*, and now he's offering me his hand in a polite gesture? I'm confused. Is this a way to lure me into a false sense of security so I don't go straight to the police should he decide to let me go one day? Why is he all of a sudden being nice to me and acting like he's trying to become friends?

Reluctantly, I take his hand in mine. As soon as our fingers meet, I feel my body relax a tiny bit, as if he's sending me calming vibes. I want to believe that he's a nice guy, and he does seem like it, but I also need to be careful when it comes to hope.

"Rosabelle," I say.

"Nice to meet you, officially. I'll have some extra blankets brought down for you. It can get cold in here at night."

"Thanks," I mutter.

This time, when he begins to walk away, I let him. I can feel the tears forming again, and I would like to cry in private for the first time tonight, rather than in a room full of pig-headed men.

Dejectedly wandering over to the bed, I lift the blanket to my nose, praying it doesn't smell old and musty. I brace myself for a worse smelling version of this dank basement that I am in and inhale lightly. I'm shocked by the smell of roses that wafts into my nose.

The pleasant smell relaxes my body, or perhaps my body is finally crashing in response to the over-stimulating events of today. I climb on top of the bed and settle myself with my back against the wall. I don't know how long I sit there sobbing through my grief, but eventually, I lull myself into slumber.

CHAPTER SEVEN
The Beast

WHAT A FUCKING NIGHT THIS HAS BEEN.
I rub my fatigue-filled eyes as I watch over the club from the catwalk above it. It feels like a week has passed since I found out about the theft. It's hard to believe it was only last night, but at least the loose ends are tied up, for now.

Reggie, the money-skimming scoundrel, is currently sinking to the depths of the ocean at the base of the cliff La Tour sits on. We made it look like he was some drunk asshole walking near the edge and fell off of it, just in case the bastard washes up anywhere. We lucked out that it was dark; Cohen's body shape and size are similar to Reggie's, so the dark silhouette wobbling across the screen on the security footage will be believable.

Mauro is out of my club for good. No more will that cheap, sloppy-ass, good-for-nothing, drunk vagabond, who doesn't know how to keep his motherfucking hands off of what doesn't belong to him, be invading in my space.

And the biggest shock of all, I've got my little lamb in a cell in the basement. When I told Dex to bring me Mauro's most prized possessions, I never expected that they would show up with a person, let alone *her*. I'm still not sure what I am going to do about her, yet. I know I'm a piece of shit for locking her away, but I need to make sure she's not a flight risk before I let her roam around freely. I can't have her running off to find her toxic Daddy.

He'll only clip her wings, whereas I wish to make her fly.

My eyes land on Cohen, beneath me on Le Côté Débutant. He's in the middle of playing with two girls who are positioned on a leather chaise in front of him, both of them on their hands and knees. Their heads are down, leaving their asses high in the air on full display for his taking.

He flogs each of the girls, in turn. Between lashes, he presses his lips to their backsides and kisses away the sting, giving them the pleasure they deserve for withstanding the pain he's inflicted. His tongue darts out, licking the juices from the slit of one of the girls, while finger fucking the other one.

He doesn't reward them for long before he's upright and flogging them once again. He looks around the club for a brief moment and his glance lands on me. He nods in my direction, silently asking me if I'm okay. I answer with a nod of my own before rearranging my hardened cock and walking to the other end of the catwalk. I can't lose track of the day-to-day business items that I usually complete on Mondays. Just because I killed one person and kidnapped another, doesn't mean the inventory is going to count itself. When I get to my office, I open the drawer to grab my clipboard, but it's not there.

"Looking for this?"

I turn at the sound of Luca in my doorway. He holds my clipboard out to me and I notice the completed inventory manifest on the top.

"What's this?"

"This week's inventory. I thought I would take care of it for you since you have your hands full with..." he pauses, pursing his lips and searching for the right phrase, "other things."

Smooth.

"What are you talking about, 'other things'?"

Exasperated by my horrible attempt to play dumb, he closes the door and sits in the chair in front of my desk.

"Adam, we've been friends for far too long for your ridiculous games to work on me," he says, bluntly.

I hate it when he calls me Adam. It means that he's trying to have a serious conversation. He's right, though.

"Fine. Thanks for doing the inventory," I say, appreciatively.

I walk around my desk and take a seat in the oversized, wingback chair that sits behind it.

"So, what's your plan?"

"I don't know, I was thinking about going home, beating off, and getting some shut-eye.

You?"

"You can't keep her locked down there forever, you know."

"I fucking know that," I answer him. "She's going to stay at Le Château."

"You're taking her home with you?"

"You got a better suggestion? You said it yourself, I can't leave her down there. You want me to put her up in a fucking playroom in Le Couloir?"

"You're dead-fucking-serious about keeping her, aren't you?" Luca knows that I do what I say I'm going to do. For him to ask me is a waste of fucking time.

"Did I say I was?"

He opens his mouth to respond, furrows his eyebrows, and closes his mouth again. Fuck. A speechless Luca isn't a good sign. Usually, he never shuts up. We're interrupted by a knock on the door. *Thank God*. I don't want to talk to anyone, but I especially don't want to sit in my own goddamn office across from a judgy Luca for much longer.

"Come in," I shout, a little too eagerly.

Cohen sticks his head into my office and

Luca finds his voice again.

"Cohen, *so* glad you're here. Come in, sit down."

"Did someone spike your coffee with coke again, Luc?"

"Fuck off," he jokes. "No, I need your assistance. Please help me explain to this fucker why keeping that girl, *for real*, is a fucking batshit crazy thing to do."

"Beast," he responds with consternation thick in his voice.

That's all he can say as he joins ranks with Luca, and they continue to stare at me in shock.

"You don't think her father has already gone to the police about this?" Cohen asks after a minute.

"No, actually, I don't. He's an imbécile who only cares about himself. I would bet the deed to La Tour that he went straight to a bar and drank until he passed out."

"So, what are you going to do?"

"I'm not sure yet. I'm still trying to figure that out. I'll tell you one thing though, after Viv I never thought I would think twice about another woman. I couldn't imagine having, *craving*, another full-time sub ever again; until I laid eyes on her."

"Holy shit," Luca gasps.

"You're serious?" Cohen questions, at the same time.

I remain silent, but I move my gaze back and forth between them. I respond by cocking my eyebrow, confirming what I just told them to be true. You would have thought these motherfuckers were celebrating me losing my virginity all over again, with the way they break out into cheers.

"Fuck off, both of you," I shout over their hooting and hollering.

"Sorry, man. But, seriously," Luca says as they both quiet down, "We never thought this day would happen either. You need this, and if this chick can give it to you, no pun intended, then we're on your side, *mon pote*!"

"We're not 12 anymore, don't call me 'buddy'," I roll my eyes at him.

"Yeah Luca, take it down a notch or three," Cohen snaps at him before turning his attention back on me. "We're happy for you, Adam."

These two have been with me through

everything since we were kids. I'm not a sentimental person, but I love them like the brothers that they've grown to be. When my parents abandoned me, they brought me into their families. When Viv was murdered, they never gave up on me. Not even when I begged them to. Not even when I was the world's biggest dickhead, and I would pick fights with them, giving them every reason to kick my ass to the curb and turn their backs on me.

After our little pow-wow, Cohen leaves to go back to the club floor to assist the Moniteurs de Dungeon in overseeing tonight's crowd, and I send Luca home to be with his sub. I need to be getting home soon too, but there's something I need to do first. I pull up the security feeds on my computer and shuffle through them until I find the one I'm looking for.

"Rosabelle," I say her name out loud for the first time.

There is no one around for me to hide from, least of all her. Her name is as beautiful as she is and I like the way it sounds as it rolls off my tongue. I can see her still form on the bed. Is she sleeping? Probably, since it's nearly two in the morning. Is she crying? Is she heartbroken? Am I the cause of her pain, or is her father?

After a short while of monitoring her from afar on the footage, I decide that I need a closer look and I make my way down to the dungeons. I settle myself on the stone seat just outside of her cell. I've been watching her carefully for the past ten minutes, matching my breathing to hers. When sleeping she looks as innocent as I'm certain she is. Not as feisty as when she's awake. In her sleep she doesn't have anyone to take care of, nothing to prove. I know all too well how it feels when you're forced to parent a parent. I know what it's like to want nothing from them but their loving care, only to get shit on and forgotten.

Before I realize what I'm doing, I'm inside of her cell. The floral scent that wafts from her as I creep closer toward her bed, titillates my senses. It turns me on and petrifies me at the same time. Can I bring her into my life like I want to? Can I come to care for someone again, and take the risk that they'll be torn from my life in a split second? I don't think I can do it.

Remembering back to the last day I spent

with Viv, I recall the feeling of her hair in my hands and her neck beneath my lips. We'd been together for years and she made me believe that I was a good person. She made me want to be the person that she saw deep inside me. It should have been me they murdered that night, not her.

Never her.

She was too pure, a fucking saint to be able to tolerate a fuck-up, dirtbag like me. I had a ring burning a hole in my pocket and I was going to give it to her at dinner that night. The dinner that we never made it to. All it took was one shot, a professional hit, for my entire world to sink back into nothingness.

Bang.

A chill runs up my spine and I shake my head to clear the unwanted trip down memory lane from my head. I hear my prisoner shiver at the same time as if she were sharing the moment with me. For an instant, I'd forgotten that she was here.

I shouldn't bring her into the mess that is my life because it could easily cost her her own. But being the kind of bastard that I am, I'm not going to change my course. I reach down and pull the blanket over her, so it covers her shoulders. Unconsciously, her hands find the hem of the blanket and she balls the fabric together in her fists and pulls it up to rest just beneath her chin.

My attention is stolen by the gleam of a ruby, shining from her right-hand ring finger. It's exquisite, just like her. The bright red stone rises from the center, with dark green emeralds set into the band. They encircle the gem, twisting around it like vines to create the shape of a rose. The gold band has seen better days, the metal is tarnished and looks though it hasn't been polished in years.

Gently, I peel her fingers from the blanket and pry open her hand. She doesn't stir. The ring doesn't fit snug around her finger, and it's easy for me to remove it.

It looks expensive and I wonder how she came by it, not that she isn't worthy of such decadence. Why didn't she offer it as part of the money that was owed by her father? It must be worth more to her than her freedom. I slip the delicate piece of jewelry into my pocket and exit her cell.

CHAPTER EIGHT

"**G**OOD MORNING, ROSABELLE!" I'M shocked awake by an extremely bubbly, very unwelcome voice in my room.

I rub the sleep from my eyes and look around. I'm not in my room, I'm in the fucking prison cell that I was forced into last night.

Fuck. It wasn't just a nightmare. I want to cry.

"I'm Paige. I've been asked to show you to your new living quarters."

I stare at the gorgeous, young woman standing in front of me. I would usually feel intimidated by someone as pretty as she is, but something about her tells me she is genuinely nice and kind. She has long dirty blonde hair that falls just below her shoulders, and warm brown eyes that remind me of espresso.

I am caught off guard by her outfit though. She is wearing a delicate, longline bra made of black lace. The fabric just under her breasts extends down further than a normal bra, but it doesn't cover her entire torso the way a corset would, and leaves her flat stomach exposed. It's paired with a short piece of black, flowy material that could hardly be considered a skirt. She is one of the most adorable women that I've ever seen. She's petite, but you can tell that what she lacks in size she makes up for in personality.

"New living quarters? I thought I was to stay here."

"I guess you can if you want," she shrugs at my question.

"No!" I offer her a genuine smile, surprising myself, but her aura is soothing and her presence eases my anxiety.

"Good girl. Let's go!"

She turns on her heel and walks from my cell. It's then I notice the lacy underwear that she has on underneath of her skirt, barely covering her ass. Both her hair and her short skirt swish through the air behind her as she walks a step ahead of me.

"Tell me about yourself, Rosabelle," she says, leading me up a short set of stairs midway along the stone corridor.

"I..." I'm thrown off by the normalcy of the conversation, taking place in the middle of the most abnormal situation that I could have ever imagined myself in. "There's really not much to say."

"Oh, come on. I find that hard to believe. You look like a fun, smart woman!" She links her arm in mine like we're best of friends.

"Thanks," I flash her a stiff smile.

"And you're stunning! All the guys are going to *love* you," she adds on, stopping me in my tracks.

"W-what guys?" I stammer.

"In the club!"

"The club? I'm not--" I stop talking.

Does she think that I applied for a job? Maybe she doesn't know why I'm here. I don't want to get either of us in trouble by giving away any information that shouldn't be divulged.

I don't know how The Beast usually handles his

kidnappings.

I roll my eyes sarcastically, trying to keep Paige from seeing me.

"You won't need to worry about them though, they know better than to go after something that belongs to Master B."

Her words hit me hard. I'm not upset to hear that no one will 'go after me'. To hear her reaffirm that I *belong to* the one everyone refers to simply as "The Beast", is a punch in the gut. *Does* she know the truth about my situation? I guess it would make sense for me to work in the club in order to pay off my father's debt, but I can't even begin to think about what job he has in mind for me.

"So, I'll be living somewhere in La Tour?"

"No, La Tour is club space only. I'm taking you to Le Château."

"Le Château?"

"Yes, did Master B not tell you? He's *horrible* when it comes to communication."

I stop walking and remove my arm from hers. She turns with a confused look on her face.

"Do you know why I am here?"

She regards me carefully, as if she's trying

not to cause me any further pain.

"I do, and I am very sorry for your circumstances. I imagine you're scared and have a thousand different questions. Let's get you to your room and we can talk about it, okay?"

I welcome the tears of relief caused by her words. She knows. Maybe that means I won't be completely alone here. My hopes are quickly dashed by the next thought that crosses my mind. She *knows*. She knows and she is going along with what The Beast has planned for me, rather than helping me escape.

Paige escorts me up a final, steep, stone staircase and through a heavy, old wooden door. The metal brackets that hold it in place squeal as she opens it. My eyes are forced closed by the bright sun that shines directly on my face. She leads me through the doorway and outside, into one of the most beautiful courtyards that I've ever seen. There is a vast expanse of vivid, soft green grass leading from the base of Le Château to the edge of the cliff that it sits on.

As we walk further into the courtyard, I spot a rose garden and my breath is stolen away by its beauty. Roses were my mother's favorite.

It's how I got my name.

Habitually, I move my thumb to my ring finger, so I can run it over the smooth gold band of my mother's ring like I often do. The happiness I felt when I first stepped foot outside is quickly dashed at the absence of the hard, metal band. I gasp suddenly and look at my right hand.

"What's wrong?" Paige looks at me with worry.

"My mother's ring is gone! I had it on when I fell asleep last night! I need to go back; I have to look for it!" I cry out.

Shit! I've never had it resized because it cost too much money. Every time I would save for it, I would need to use the money for a house or car repair.

"We can't right now, we're on a strict schedule, I'm sorry."

"What? No! We have to! Please!"

"Oh, don't fret, we will find it. I promise you, as soon as we get to Le Château, I will send word that it needs to be found."

"Someone might steal it!"

"The Beast won't let that happen, trust me.

He doesn't tolerate stealing."

Her statement hits me like another punch in the gut and she suddenly realizes her poor choice of words.

"Yeah, tell me something I don't know," I grimace, looking away from her.

"Rosabelle, I'm so sorry. I didn't think before I opened my mouth."

"It's fine. It's not *your* fault that I'm here."

"Come on, we don't want to be late."

Paige begins walking again and I fall silently in line behind her.

During the remainder of our journey, Paige explains to me that The Beast lives in Le Château. *Of course, he does.* He seems to be ostentatious by nature; the club is proof enough of that. I was happy to hear that both her and Luca live there too. I'd like to think that it will be a little easier being here, with her nearby.

"Here we are," Paige reaches for the doorknob in front of her and opens the door into one of the most beautiful rooms I've ever seen.

When I pictured where I would live or sleep during my imprisonment, I never imagined anything like the room that I am standing in right now. I make no exaggeration when I say that it's larger than my entire house. A pang of longing pierces my heart when thinking of home. I don't care how beautiful or decadent this place is, it's not mine.

"It's so beautiful. I've never seen anything as grand as this. To be honest I am curious why that monster wants me, his *prisoner*, staying in such a lavish, ridiculously gorgeous room."

It's brightly decorated in royal blue and yellow. It's welcoming and warm. The large four-poster bed is inviting, and I wonder if it feels as soft and grand as it looks. There is a white, tufted bench at the end of the bed, a table and two chairs off to the right, just beneath a large window. I notice a balcony on the other side of the glass. Did he ask her to show this to me, to dangle it in front of me, just for him to take it away, like the cruel beast he is?

"You can't think of yourself as a prisoner or you will never make it, Rosabelle. It's time to embrace your new life. It's going to be a challenge, but I can tell that you're very brave, and I'll be here for you."

Paige truly does seem like a good person. It leads me to wonder if her and Luca are also prisoners of The Beast. Maybe that's why they haven't opted to help me escape. They both seem happy. Are they here because they want to be, or have they accepted their fate as I should mine?

"Your en suite is through that door there." she waves her hand in the direction of the bathroom and I pad across the floor to it.

Once again, I am shocked by the size of the room that I am in.

"I'll get your bath started and help to prepare you for Master B."

"I'm sorry, what?"

"He's provided me with a specific set of instructions detailing how he would like you prepared."

She says this as she walks to the bathtub and twists the faucets, letting the water flow into the large, clawfoot tub situated beneath it.

"*Prepared*? What is he going to do, eat me?"

"Only if you're a good girl," she says, flashing me a sly smile.

My eyes go wide as I finally realize what my fate is going to be. He's letting me stay in this extravagant room in exchange for myself. All of me, even the pieces that I am not willing to give.

"When you said you know my situation, what is it that you know?"

"That you've agreed to be Master B's new submissive."

She looks at me like I'm crazy. Like I should know what she's talking about. My knees go weak and I feel as though I am going to fall over.

"No! I never said…"

I think back to our discussion last night.

"If you do this, there's no taking it back. You will be mine…forever."

"I know."

Oh my God, I never thought that this is what he meant when he uttered those words.

"That's not what I meant! I'll gladly go back to the dungeon to wither away and die, than have that horrid beast touch me!"

"No, it's not like--"

I don't hear the rest of what Paige says as

I run out of the bathroom and tear open the door into the hallway. The left is a dead-end so I quickly turn around and run off to the right. I can hear Paige behind me, shouting for me to come back. I push myself harder, to run faster. There is another corridor at the end of this one, where I can either go left or right. I'm trying to remember which way we came from, so I can find my way back outside and attempt to get out of here.

I turn my head to see if Paige is gaining on me. I'm relieved to see she's still too far back to catch me, but the feeling vanishes when I look ahead again and see the mammoth form of The Beast blocking me from reaching the next corridor. I slow as quickly as possible and look back and forth between him and Paige.

Fuck!

He storms forward with a menacing look on his face, rooting me to my spot in fear. When he reaches me, I brace myself for… I don't know what for. Will he hit me? Scream at me? Fuck me?

I shake with terror as his hand closes around my throat. He forces me backward into the wall behind me, just like he did in La Tour the other night.

And just like the other night, an unwelcome ache begins to grow deep inside of me.

"What the *fuck* do you think you're doing?"

"Master B, I'm sorry, I--" Paige catches up with us and tries to explain what happened.

The Beast never takes his eyes off of me. Instead, he holds his hand up, quieting her and points to the floor. In an instant, she is kneeling with her legs spread wide, her hands behind her back, her eyes on the ground.

"She--" I begin to defend Paige, but I'm trembling too much to get the words out.

"She what, little lamb?" he asks with intensity burning in his eyes.

"She didn't do anything wrong," I manage to get out. It's difficult to talk with his large hand around my throat. "She doesn't deserve to get into trouble."

"She's not my problem, you are."

He pulls me away from the wall and guides me down the corridor, still with a strong hold on the back of my neck.

"Paige," he says to her over his shoulder,

"Find Master Luca and explain what happened. He can decide if you need to be punished or not."

"Thank you, Sir," I hear her say from behind us.

Paige is a sub? That would explain her outfit. When we get back into the room that I just escaped from, he pushes me into the center of it and slams the door behind us, breathing heavily. My eyes never leave him. I'm terrified when he moves toward me again.

"I won't repeat myself. Start talking," he commands, referring to the question he asked me in the corridor.

"I refuse to be your sex slave!" I say, lacking all of the bravado that I was trying to display in my voice.

An evil grin spreads across his face.

"I'll gladly go back down to the dungeon. I'd rather stay there for the rest of my life than be forced to do something that I don't want to do."

"First of all, little lamb, you don't *refuse* me. You belong to me now. You knew what you were getting into when you foolishly traded your life for your father's."

He stalks toward me and I back up slowly, stopping only when my legs hit the side of the bed. I turn my head to escape his taunting stare. But, if I'm being completely honest with myself, I'm turning away to escape the feeling that is certain to reignite the moment our eyes lock.

"Secondly, I don't want you as a sex slave." he continues toward me and in a matter of seconds his body is pressed up against mine. He grabs a fistful of my hair and tugs my head back, forcing my eyes to meet his, "So don't flatter yourself."

"You--you don't?" I ask, immediately annoyed at myself for sounding hurt.

"No. I would *never* touch someone who didn't want to be touched or force them to do something that they don't want to do; that's not my kind of kink. But I can *promise* you, it won't be long until you're *begging* for my touch."

"I'll never beg you for anything," I respond defiantly and pray that my shaky voice doesn't give away the desire I'm fighting to hide.

Why does he affect me like this?

"Never say never, little lamb."

He releases his hold on me and walks into the bathroom, starting the water. My eyes flit to the bedroom door and I consider running again.

"You can think about running all you'd like, but you'll never be free from me."

My attention whips back to him. He's leaning against the wall next to the bathtub, challenging me.

"I think I'll stay here while you wash up, just in case you feel the need to flee again."

When he feels confident that I'm not going anywhere, he walks to another part of the bathroom out of sight from where I am.

"Come."

I don't want to give into him, but my legs don't seem to care. I push off the side of the bed and saunter into the bathroom, with my arms crossed in front of me. I look for him in the room when I don't immediately see him, and see that he's in a gigantic dressing closet full of clothing and shoes.

"How in the…" I question, wondering how he was able to fill a closet of this size overnight.

"The bath products that you're to use are on the ledge of the tub. I want you shaved, thoroughly. When you're finished come back here and I'll show you what you're to wear for the day. Get started."

"But--,"

"Now." he looks up from the drawer that he's searching in, and stares at me seriously.

The last thing I want is to be naked anywhere near him, but his sinister tone is back and I decide not to provoke him any further. At least he isn't making me strip in front of him. I exit the dressing closet. Thankfully, the bathtub can't be seen from inside there. I pick up the soap and squeeze some into the running water. I add more than I normally would, because the more bubbles there are, the better.

I watch the doorway carefully as I get undressed, and once the last item of clothing is off, I quickly climb over the ledge and into the tub, making a slight splash.

I lay my body back, resting on the smooth porcelain. I don't want to enjoy anything of his, but I can't deny that this feels incredible. Lying back, I close my eyes and take a deep breath, letting the hot water relax me. I recite my mantra in my head, the one that always helps me feel better in stressful or painful situations.

I am smart, strong, and independent. I am beautiful. I am proud to be me. I can overcome any obstacle in my path, and that is what I will do to survive; as I always have.

I'm lost in my moment when I'm suddenly startled by his voice. I open my eyes to see him standing over me.

CHAPTER NINE
The Beast

I GATHER THE CLOTHING THAT SHE WILL WEAR for her training today. She's not going to like what I've picked out, and I'm sure she'll try to fight me, but I don't care. Once she realizes it's the same outfit that Paige is wearing, she should relax a little bit. And if she doesn't, I'll help her relax. I was truthful when I told her that I wouldn't force anyone to do something that they don't want to do. But, I *know* there are things that she'd like to do; things that she would never admit to. I've seen it every time I've looked into her stunning hazel eyes. I just need to get her on the club floor and see which activity makes her face light up the most. I'm not above manipulating her into trying new things.

I hear a loud splash in the bathroom and I peek my head out to see what's going on and whether or not she is obeying my instructions. I'm surprised when I see the top of her head just over the edge of the bathtub.

Good girl.

When everything is laid out, I walk into the bathroom to find her lying back in the tub with her eyes closed. She is underneath one of the largest mountains of bubbles I've ever seen. I steal a moment to stare at her. She is even more beautiful with fewer clothes on. I can just make out where the curve of her tits begin, before they disappear beneath the bubbles, and the temptation drives me wild. Though I am pleased that she listened, I'm irritated that I can't see more of her.

All in good time.

"This isn't the spa, hurry up," I command.

I'm amused to see I've startled her. She covers herself before sitting up straight.

"I can't do this with you standing here watching me,"

"I'm not leaving, I can't risk you trying to

run again."

I pick her clothes up off the floor. She looks like she's going to object to my doing so, but she doesn't. Not even when I throw them in the trash can.

She scowls at me as she reaches for the cup on the ledge of the tub while keeping her other arm over her tits, so I can't see them. She sticks the cup in the water to fill it. I wonder what she's doing until she lifts it and pours it over her head. She places the cup back and feels her hair to see if it's all wet. Then, she picks it up again.

Watching her, learning her mannerisms and quirks, fascinates me. She's adorable, strong, intelligent, stubborn. Being a witness to her bathing herself turns me on more than I've been in a long time, but I almost wish she didn't know that I was here. She could be herself and not this meek version of the wild beauty that I know is inside of her.

Once all of her hair is soaking wet, she places the cup back on the ledge and reaches for the shampoo, but I get to it first.

"Hey! I'm doing what you asked!"

I know you are, little lamb, but I can't just stand

by and watch any longer.

The need to bathe her, to care for what's mine, nags at my soul. My true nature is begging to be released. I can't let him out completely, yet, but a small piece of him will be fine.

"You have an appointment in an hour and I don't tolerate tardiness. At the rate you're going, you won't be finished until tomorrow. If you can't bathe yourself properly, then you're going to force me to step in."

"I know how to bathe myself properly!"

"Then why weren't you?"

"How am I supposed to do that? I've been *kidnapped* and forced to bathe in front of a complete stranger."

"Wrong again. Remember, this was your idea, and you chose to be here. Don't try to turn this around."

"Like I really had a choice?!" she screeches.

She gasps when I grab her by the hair and force her to look into my eyes.

"There is *always* a choice," I bark.

Her words infuriate me.

My parents had a choice to be present in my life, to make me feel loved and wanted. To include me in their grand plan, but they chose adventure, drugs, and their mistress over me. The evil murderer who killed Viv had a choice. They could have killed me and spared her, allowing her to continue to shine and brighten the lives of everyone around her. Instead, they chose to condemn me to a life of darkness.

I can't seem to tear my gaze away from her. I hold her in place for a moment longer than I intended to because her stare calms me slightly.

"Sit still," I command her, letting go of her hair.

She pulls her legs up to her chest and wraps her arms around them. Her sideboob is accentuated by the force of her legs squishing her tits. She would hate that I can see it, but I'm certainly not going to tell her. My cock hardens and pushes painfully against the zipper of my pants.

"What kind of appointment?" she asks.

"You'll find out when you get there."

She sighs heavily and pouts as I squeeze some shampoo onto my palm and rub it into her silky, chestnut brown hair.

"You need to relax," I tell her.

"I can't do that with you in here, especially when you're yelling at me and pulling my hair."

"A lot of women like having their hair pulled," I taunt her.

"Well, I'm not a lot of women."

No, you're not.

I wonder if she's a virgin. If not, how many guys has she slept with? One? Two? More? No. Two, maybe, but I'm guessing no more than that. My little lamb is virtuous.

Grabbing the cup from the ledge, I fill it with water and rinse the shampoo from her hair. I repeat the process with the conditioner and once I've made sure that all of it is out, I stand and bring her a towel.

"Use the soap to wash your body thoroughly. Don't forget to shave. I'll be right back."

I don't miss the daggers that she shoots my way as I enter the dressing closet and adjust my cock. I'm hard as a fucking rock. Taking care of her like this brings back a lot of painful memories. I don't even know what I'm still doing in here. I lied about needing to be here so she wouldn't try running away again. I could have easily just locked her in her room.

I need to get out of here and try to fucking compose myself before her training session. I open my cell phone and shoot Luca a text asking if Paige is allowed to help Rosabelle again. I doubt he punished her, but I won't make assumptions about what goes on between another Dom and his sub. He responds almost immediately, telling me that she is on her way.

I peek into the bathroom and find Rosabelle with one leg up on the side of the tub, razor in hand. I can't believe I'm hiding in here, what the fuck is wrong with me? Fucking pathetic. Why do I care if she knows I'm looking? I'll look at her whenever I damn well please and she can learn to like it.

I give her a few more minutes before checking on her again. When I do, I catch a glimpse of her perfectly round ass. Just before she wraps a towel around herself, I exit the closet. Within seconds, I hear Paige calling her name from the bedroom.

"Wait here. Paige will be in to help you in a second." I pass Rosabelle, still standing in the bathtub, fumbling to get the towel around herself before I can see her body.

Too late.

"Nice ass, by the way."

"Hey!" I hear her exclaim, but I don't acknowledge it.

When I exit the bathroom, Paige is standing just inside the doorway.

"I don't think she'll run again but if she does, know that you won't be to blame for it."

"Yes, Sir," she acknowledges.

"I've laid out her training uniform, please have her dressed and downstairs on time. Lunch will be here shortly. If there are any problems, contact Luca."

"Yes, Sir."

"Thank you, Paige."

CHAPTER TEN
Rosabelle

RELIEF WASHES OVER ME AS THE BEAST LEAVES the bathroom and tells me that Paige will be coming back. I thought he was going to stay here and watch me get dressed. I pat my body dry with the towel and wait for further instruction.

Taking in my surroundings again, I think about how I might feel if my circumstances were different. If I were here willingly. I don't care what The Beast said, I didn't have a choice. I would never have allowed my father's life to be taken when I could offer my own. Regardless of the reason I came to be at Le Château, I will never feel as though I belong. With its gorgeous, intricate details and lavish furnishings, it's everything I'm not.

But when I think about my home, my job, I never felt like I fit in there either. I get along with people, mostly, but I don't have anyone in my life that I would really call a friend.

Will I ever feel like I belong anywhere?

My thoughts are interrupted by a light knock on the doorframe. I look up and see Paige, waiting for me to invite her in.

"Hi," I say to her with a relieved smile. "You can come in. I'm so sorry if I got you into any trouble earlier."

"Oh, everything is fine, don't worry. Come on into the closet and I'll go over what's going to happen next."

I immediately begin to feel nervous again.

"Master B said he laid your clothes out...ah, there they are!"

She walks around the set of drawers in the middle of the closet and picks up what appears to be scraps of fabric.

"Go ahead and put these on." She hands them to me.

I turn from her and attempt to keep the towel from falling off me as I place the clothing down, trying to make sense out of it.

"Rosabelle, don't be so shy."

"Hmm?" I turn around and shoot her a confused look. "What do you mean?"

"We're both girls, you can drop the towel so it's easier for you to get dressed."

"Oh."

I close my eyes and take a deep breath, dropping the towel. Paige doesn't say anything and just before I force my eyes open, I hear her stand up and walk behind me. She places her hands on my shoulders and speaks again.

"You can open your eyes, Rosabelle. Relax, you don't have anything that I haven't seen before."

She nudges me toward the full-length mirror, forcing me to look at myself. My body flushes with embarrassment.

"You have a gorgeous body, and you're very sexy when you blush."

Her words shock me and I raise my eyes to hers through the reflection of the mirror.

"But you shouldn't be shy, the female body is a work of art to be appreciated, Rosabelle. To be worshipped. Trust me when I tell you, that

Master B is going to worship the *fuck* out of you."

Once again, my body is flooded with bashfulness.

Or is it lust?

"Oh, but not with that bush. Did Master B not tell you that he wanted you shaved?"

"He told me to shave thoroughly. I didn't realize that's what he meant."

"Hmm," Paige says, making me nervous again.

"What?"

"Nothing," she starts, "I guess I'm surprised that he didn't do it for you, that's all."

She shoots me a sly smile. I don't even know what to say about that, so I don't say anything. I can barely imagine the thought of shaving down there, let alone having someone do it for me.

"Let's go," she says, pointing to the bathroom. "Back to the tub."

"I can't do this, Paige."

I'm standing in the mirror staring at my

completely smooth body as if it's the first time I've ever looked at myself naked. I feel like a child! Paige supervised while I learned how to shave my 'pussy', as she put it. She wouldn't let me use the words pubic hair; apparently, it's a turn-off. She also told me that 'pussy' should never be considered a bad word.

"It's female empowerment, Rosabelle! Embrace it!"

"Come sit," she says to me, patting the space next to her on the tufted ottoman against the wall.

"You are a very smart girl. I can see it, Master Luca can see it, and Master B can see it. You know what goes on in La Tour. You knew, when you traded your life for your father's, that your world was going to change, right?"

Tears form in my eyes at her words. Everything she's saying is true and no matter how badly I don't want to accept it, I know it's not going away.

"I know this sounds ridiculous, but I didn't realize *this* is what he meant when he said I would be *his.* This lifestyle, it's not like anything I've ever experienced before. The riches are overwhelming enough, but when I think about what else is going to be expected of me… it paralyzes me with fear."

"I understand your apprehension. It's not easy and no one is going to throw you into a situation that you aren't ready for. Something that people who are on the outside don't understand, is that with submission comes freedom. It sounds backward, but to have someone to entrust with your choices, knowing that they have your best interests at heart, is one of the most intoxicating feelings I've ever experienced."

I want to believe what she's saying, but I can't wrap my head around it.

"The idea that I can finally relax and not have to worry about my father, my job, money, bills, everything, does sound incredible. But I can't wrap my head around what I will have to sacrifice in order to experience that."

"Who says you're going to sacrifice anything?"

I stare at her, confused.

"When you're with your Dom, you'll never feel like you're sacrificing part of yourself to him. Trust me. I was nervous coming here, too. I was out of options; I didn't have a home, a family, and I was nothing. Master Luca took me in as an esclave de maison about three years ago. I was terrified of being someone's *toy*, a thing for them to use, but I quickly realized that's not what being a submissive is about."

I look at her in disbelief.

"Well, that's not *all* that it's about. Don't knock it 'til you try it, that part is fun, too. You just need to open your mind a little."

She takes in my skeptical expression and continues.

"When I met Master Luca, he showed me what desire truly meant. Yes, he desired me sexually. But I learned that he also had a strong desire to care for me, to protect me, to ensure my happiness. It didn't take long for me to see that he cherished me. I can tell that you are a strong and independent person, Rosabelle. Becoming a submissive doesn't mean you have to give up those qualities."

"I can understand that, to an extent, but I can't get over the idea that The Beast expects to snap his fingers and make me perform."

"That's not what it's going to be like. It will be much easier to show you than to tell you. Let's finish getting dressed. Lunch will be ready soon and we have to be downstairs in less than an hour."

"This would be a lot easier if I looked like you in this outfit, Paige. I can't pull this off. I feel like a fraud!"

"Rosabelle, you look stunning! Believe me when I tell you that. Just wait until Master B sees you."

"That's the problem, he's the *last* person I want to see me like this."

"You really ought to try and give him a chance. He's not the horrible monster you're imagining."

I roll my eyes, but find myself considering what she said. She's got me thinking about when The Beast was washing my hair. He was tender. His gentle touch was as unexpected as the craving my body had for him.

He could have shaved me himself, as Paige

explained. He could have done a *lot* of things to me, but he didn't. Does he feel the same connection that I do when his eyes meet mine? If not, why would he be so adamant about making me his submissive? Maybe he thinks that I *don't* feel the connection.

"Earth to Rosabelle."

Paige breaks through my train of thought as she links her arm with mine like she did this morning. I smile at her and let her lead me from my bedroom. I can feel the hem of my skirt tickling my thighs just under the curve of my ass. I take a deep breath and remind myself that I am strong and can make it through anything life throws at me. I replay Paige's words in my head, 'With submission comes freedom.'

The walk to La Tour doesn't take as long as I hoped it would. Yes, it's only located on the other side of Le Château, but I could have used a few more minutes to mentally prepare myself.

When we enter the club, we're in the corridor in the back, where The Beast and I first met. My eyes land on the spot where he held me against the wall and I feel the same dull ache forming in the pit of my stomach that was there that evening. I tried to convince myself that it was nerves, but it's foolish to kid myself any longer.

I'll give him a chance, but I vow not to lose my sense of self. I refuse to be a mindless whore who drops to her knees just because a man tells her to. If that's who The Beast wants me to be, he's got another thing coming.

CHAPTER ELEVEN
Rosabelle

MY HEART HAS NEVER BEAT AS QUICKLY AS it's beating right now. Paige went into the training room, but told me that I needed to wait outside until they called me in. I would give anything to know what they're talking about. It infuriates me to no end knowing that they're in there discussing me or my life and I am not part of the conversation.

Just as I feel myself ready to snap, the door opens wide and Paige waves me in. My feet feel like boulders, barely able to move. I look at Paige and she urges me to hurry.

When I get to the doorway, she whispers to me. "Come in and stand up straight, just inside the door. Don't raise your eyes, keep them on the floor."

I want to ask her if she came up with that rhyme herself, but I wouldn't be able to speak right now even if I were allowed to. It turns out that the fear of the unknown waiting for me in that room, vastly overpowers the embarrassment I feel about being seen in this outfit. I put one foot in front of the other and walk over the threshold. I do exactly as she says and wait by the door, keeping my eyes fixed on the floor in front of me.

"Good job, you're doing great," she whispers again before closing the door and standing next to me.

"Rosabelle."

My heart races faster at the sound of my name on his lips. It's the first time he's used it when speaking to me. I thought for sure he would call me "little lamb" again. Do I look up or do I keep my eyes down? I wait for Paige to help me out, but she remains silent.

Thanks a lot.

She calls him "Master B" when she's talking to me about him, but when she spoke directly to him earlier, she called him "Sir." The idea of using either of those terms makes my skin crawl.

Open your mind Rosabelle; step out of your comfort zone.

I force every value that I was raised on back into the furthest corner of my mind, locking them away for safekeeping, and step into the new world that I am a part of.

"Yes, Sir?"

"Come."

I turn my head a little in Paige's direction, before moving.

"With submission comes freedom," she whispers.

Her words give me just enough encouragement to get my feet moving. I pad across the floor slowly, moving in the direction of his voice. I am very thankful for the rule about keeping my eyes lowered. I don't think I would be able to move if I had to look at him. But, when I see two pairs of feet up ahead, I pause.

Who else is here? And which feet belong to The Beast?

I see one pair of feet move forward and it's as if he can read my mind.

"Here."

I continue walking until I am directly in front of him. His scent hits me and I breathe it in deeply.

"Ange."

Angel. The other man speaks and I recognize Luca's voice from the night before. I laugh inwardly at the revelation. With Paige here, I should have known the other pair of feet belonged to Luca.

"Good girl. Have a seat."

I watch Paige out of the corner of my eye as she kneels on the floor, in the same way she did in the hallway outside of my bedroom. Legs spread, hands behind her back. Her eyes are still focused on the floor. I see The Beast's hand come into view and he places it under my chin. He gently lifts my face to meet his gaze. My eyes bore into his for a moment before I begin to feel uncomfortable and need to look away.

"Look at me. Keep your eyes forward."

I comply with his request.

"Good girl."

I wait for his choice of praise to anger me, but it doesn't. Would it have if Luca hadn't said it to Paige first? I don't have time to think about it because a second later he begins to look my body up and down, assessing me thoroughly. I stand there, hating life, cursing Paige for feeding me a crock full of lies. Having someone walk circles around you, critiquing you, looking for any flaw that you may have, and knowing they're going to find several. This is an awful, uncomfortable feeling. I fight the urge to run from the room with every second that I'm left waiting, dreading what he is going to say when he finally speaks.

"You're exquisite, little lamb."

Exquisite?

I feel my eyebrows furrow in disbelief. That's not at all what I was expecting to hear, but the way the timbre in his voice thickened with lust after his inspection of me, lit a flame of desire deep within me. No one has ever regarded me with such awe and respect before.

"A true beauty," he says as he stops in front of me.

I don't know what to say to that.

"This is where you would say, 'Thank you, Sir.'"

It's a lot harder addressing him when I am

looking at him. I clear my throat.

"Thank you, Sir."

The corners of his lips twitch into a smug grin.

Bastard!

"Have a seat."

I kneel on the ground and position my body exactly how Paige's is. Once I'm down, The Beast and Luca walk over to the far side of the room. I turn my head, curious to see where they're going and watch as they open a closet that's situated there.

"Rosabelle," I hear Paige whisper scream from the opposite direction, "Eyes down."

I turn my eyes back to the floor before I can see what is in the closet. I can probably guess though. We're in a training room in the middle of a sex club.

"You're doing great, by the way. Keep it up!"

"Paige!"

Luca's voice echos off the walls of the room. Oh, shit. How did he hear her talking from way over there?

"Come," he commands, pointing to a chair

next to him.

I blanch when I see her begin crawling to meet him. I will never be okay with obeying commands and acting like I'm a dog.

"I'm sorry," I say, getting up from the floor and walking toward them. "It's my fault, she was correcting me."

"Silence!" The Beast roars at me, and I am legitimately frightened. "Did I tell you to get up off of the ground?"

"No, I'm sorry. I just--"

"No, *Sir!*" he corrects me, sternly.

"No, Sir. I'm sorry," I kneel down on the ground again and continue trying to explain myself. "I did something wrong and she was just trying to help."

He stands tall over me, looking like he is going to yell. But as I look up at him from down on my knees, something stops him.

"There are rules that need to be followed. Paige knows what they are. It was her choice to speak out of turn. Do you remember the discussion that we had about choices this morning?"

I begin to nod my head, but he cocks his

eyebrow at me.

"Yes, Sir," I say.

He walks around me and crouches down, placing a hand on my shoulder, possessively.

"We weren't going to cover punishment first thing, but I guess now is as good a time as any. Master Luca?"

"Stand, slave," he begins.

"*Slave?*" I repeat, not caring whether or not I'm following their rules.

That's abhorrent. I will never be okay with anyone degrading me like that. What happened to '*Angel*'? She breaks one tiny rule so she can help someone else, and she falls from grace?

"You'll keep quiet unless you want to be next, Rosabelle," The Beast threatens, stoking the embers that burn dimly in my core.

With the attention of both The Beast as well as Luca on me, Paige uses that second to make a face, telling me to put a lid on it.

"I'm sorry. Sir." I tack on at the end, almost forgetting.

"I'm not the only one you need to apologize to. You interrupted Master Luca."

"I'm sorry," I say, bowing my head slightly.

"Sir."

"Sir! I'm sorry, Sir. *God, I'm sorry everyone!*"

I'm already feeling overwhelmed. This isn't a good sign. I swear Luca just pursed his lips like he was about to smile. Does *he* get punished for breaking character? He nods his head at me and directs his attention back to Paige.

Bringing her up into a standing position, his hand slithers up the backs of her legs and underneath her skirt. In one swift, extremely provocative motion, he rips her panties off her. Turning her around, he ties her hands behind her back with the scrap of lace. Straightening her again, so she is positioned the way he wants her, he offers his hand to her and helps her lay down, across his lap.

When she is settled in place, he lifts her tiny skirt so it's out of the way, exposing her ass to him.

"Count them out."

"Yes, Master."

I watch in awe as Luca lifts his hand and brings it down on Paige's ass cheek, the slap echoes around the room.

"One. Thank you, Sir."

He lifts his hand high, and brings it down again, this time on her other cheek.

"Two. Thank you, Sir."

Smack!

"Three. Thank you, Sir."

My stomach begins to tighten and the fire within burns hotter than before. The ache morphs into a tingle, which spreads outward from my core, sending a small rush of moisture through the slit between my legs. I tear my attention from Paige's punishment and stare down at the apex of my spread thighs.

"Head up, Rosabelle," The Beast orders me and my head shoots up to watch the scene unfolding before me again.

Smack!

"Four! Thank you, Sir."

Before I realize what I am doing, my hand moves toward the center of my legs and I have to fight to keep it from connecting with my clit.

"Five! Thank you, Sir."

Paige's voice is getting a little louder with each smack. Is she in pain? Is she excited? Both, maybe? My index finger rubs against my lower stomach, inching closer to the sensitive spot on my body that is begging to be touched.

Smack!

The sound of skin on skin and the sensual cry that escapes Paige's lips causes my stomach to tense again. My eyes widen of their own accord and a second later, I feel more moisture pool between my legs.

Smack!

I don't know whether or not to be embarrassed or excited about the fact that watching this is turning me on. This has never happened to me before. When I was with Gavin, I was never in the mood. I never got wet, unless he spit on me, and I've never had an orgasm. Not even by my own hand.

"Rosabelle," The Beast warns when he notices me getting distracted again.

"I'm sorry, Sir."

I move my hand far from where it just was. I try to pull it off as though I had an itch on the outer portion of my leg, but I don't know if it worked.

"What are you thinking about?" he asks me softly.

Oh fuck.

"Nothing. I'm just not used to seeing something like this."

"Don't lie to me, little lamb," he bends closer, whispering in my ear. "That's something that I will not tolerate."

I swallow the lump that just landed in my throat.

"Do you enjoy watching Master Luca spank Paige?"

This time he speaks loud enough for them to hear.

Smack!

"Nine! Thank you, Sir!" Paige pants and I can hear the appreciation in her voice.

She's enjoying herself and I realize that I am, too. The intimacy of what is playing out in front of me isn't as shocking as the incredible sense of eroticism I feel at watching it happen.

"Rosabelle. I meant what I said earlier. I won't repeat myself. This is your last warning."

"Yes, Sir," I finally answer him, breaking the trance that I'm in.

I swallow my pride and admit a secret desire to a complete stranger. Something that I never thought I would be asked to or be able to admit.

Smack!

"TEN! Thank you, Sir!"

The second that Luca is finished with the punishment, he begins rubbing Paige's ass cheeks, in an effort to soothe them. Why? Doesn't that negate it?

My thoughts are interrupted by the sound of The Beast's whispers in my ear, "Are you wet, little lamb?"

His question catches me off guard and I stiffen up again. What is he going to do to me if I say yes? What will he do if I lie? I consider not saying anything, but he just gave me my final warning and I know for a fact that I am not ready to find out what happens when I use them all up.

"I'm scared."

"Of what?"

"Of telling the truth. Of lying."

"You never have to be scared of telling the truth, no matter what it is. Do you understand?"

He places his hand on my cheek and turns my face to look at him. I think back to my earlier conversation with Paige. He's being serious, and not just because he wants an answer to his question, but because he wants to know how I'm feeling. Because he wants to care for me. I can see the honesty shining through his stare.

"Yes, Sir."

"And, I will never lie to you."

Tenderly, he curls a piece of hair behind my ear before speaking again.

"Besides, I already know what I'll find if I dip my finger in your pussy right now."

He traces a finger across my upper thigh, dangerously close to the place where I am not okay with him being. I feel my face flush bright red and I pull my legs together, closing them.

"Like I said, it won't be long until you beg me to touch you."

He grins like a sly fox and stands.

"Go sit, Paige," Luca commands and Paige crawls down from his lap and takes her position next to me.

I follow her lead and resituate myself, so I am back in the correct position.

"Rosabelle, you may look up as I require your full attention at this time."

I look up at The Beast, ready for his next instruction.

CHAPTER TWELVE
The Beast

I MUST SAY, MY LITTLE LAMB SURPRISES ME MORE and more every time I see her. I would have bet a million dollars that she wouldn't obey my commands right away. More than that, I was blown away when she nearly started touching herself. I almost let her, but I'm a selfish prick. If I don't get to touch her no one else does, herself included.

I'm going to need to find out what Paige said in order to get her to relax enough to come down here. Then, I need to make sure Luca thanks her properly. But we've barely even scratched the surface. So, I'm going to see how far I can push her until she really starts to squirm.

"I'm granting you an open conversation to

ask me any questions you might have regarding your new life. Whatever you'd like, but with the understanding that there will be questions that I am not going to answer. That being said, I will also be asking questions, but you are required to give me an answer. If you refuse, then you will be punished, understood?"

She makes a face and I know she wants to argue with me.

"Rosabelle," I warn her.

I can see the wheels in her head turning.

"I'd be more than happy to take you over my knee," I threaten.

Fight me, little lamb. Make me do it.

"Understood, Sir."

I manage to keep the disappointment from my face, but she's smart. I think she knows I'm hoping that she will defy me.

"Do you have any questions for me?"

"Yes, Sir."

"Go ahead," I encourage her.

"You told me this morning that you wouldn't touch someone who didn't want to be touched, and you wouldn't force them to do something that they don't want to do."

"That's correct."

"But you just said if I don't want to answer a question, you're going to *force* me to or else I will be punished. I can only assume the punishment will be in such a way that will require your *touch*. How does that work, then? Because you also just said that you don't lie."

And there she is. My feisty, little lamb.

I manage to catch Luca's and Paige's expressions; they're scared for her. And they should be. My little lamb isn't ready for what I have planned for her.

"I'm so glad you asked. Luca, Paige, you're both dismissed," I tell them. "Rosabelle, don't move from that spot." I take sadistic delight in witnessing the spread of shock and terror pass across her beautiful face.

I walk to the closet in the back of the training room and open it, looking for the items that I will need.

If she wants to touch herself now, then she can feel free. That's not me forcing her, but if she's going to do it, it's going to be for me. If she refuses, then I'll punish her, and there are a hundred ways I can do that without ever laying a finger on her.

"Beast," Luca approaches me.

I'm not surprised to see that Luca hasn't left yet. I turn around to check on my little lamb and am happy to see that she is where she belongs and that Paige has gone.

"What are you doing, man?" Luca asks.

"Answering her question."

"You've got that look in your eye, that evil gleam that scares the shit out of people. I don't know if it's a good idea for you to be alone with her right now."

"Okay, I admit that a second ago I overreacted in response to her bullshit question, but I'm not going to destroy her, just teach her a lesson."

Luca looks me dead in the eye, unsure whether or not he believes me.

"I promise."

"Fine," he finally believes me, "But you're not to leave this room with her, and I'll be in the observation area supervising you the entire time."

"Fine," I agree.

Luca leaves me at the closet and enters the

observation area through the near-by door. I grab a set of vibrating panties and a wand massager and close the closet. On my way back to where Rosabelle sits, I pull another chair over with me. I situate the chair in front of the one where Luca punished Paige *so* beautifully, that it made my little lamb so wet she nearly touched herself. She wants to let herself go.

Fuck; get your shit together. Remember who you are. I take a calming breath and think about my sub. That's what a responsible Dom does. She's the first sub I've had in three years. I can't fuck her up on her first day. She doesn't need punishment right now, she needs support; encouragement. She responded much better to me upstairs when I backed off my attitude and took charge. I take a few more breaths to center myself before acknowledging her again.

"Come."

Her reaction is a little slow for my liking, but she moves before I have to repeat myself. I'm floored when she begins to crawl to me. That's not what I meant for her to do when I gave her the order, but she's imitating what she saw Paige doing. The sight of her slinking toward me on all fours, like a kitten, drives me crazy. Maybe she needs a new nickname?

No.

She will *always* be my little lamb.

I'm glad Luca insisted on staying. Holding back may be more difficult than I originally thought. She stops when she gets to me and sits back on her heels.

"You're a fast learner, Rosabelle. That's very good. Up, in the chair."

She sits down and crosses her legs. I rest on the edge of the chair across from her, placing the toys on the floor.

"Look at me."

She listens. I can see the fear and anticipation in her eyes. I don't want her to fear me.

"I apologize for losing my temper a second ago. I'm not going to hurt you. I would never do that. As your Dom, it's my privilege and responsibility to make sure you're taken care of. Do you believe me?"

"Yes, Sir."

"Part of that is making you feel good. You've been absolutely remarkable since you walked through that door, Rosabelle. You came in here full of intrigue and with an open mind. Look at the impact of that attitude. Don't you want to see where that can take you?"

She looks at me like she isn't sure what to say.

"Are you destined to be a bored, little girl with no life because she feels responsible for a father that doesn't deserve her?"

She can't believe what I said. Not because I said it, but because it's an actual fear of hers.

"You deserve excitement, pleasure, happiness. I can help you achieve all of those things. I know how independent you are. That is one of the things that I admire the fuck out of about you, Rosabelle. But that doesn't mean that you can't let go and have someone else catch you from time to time."

She looks at me as she's deep in thought. I would give anything to know what she's thinking.

"Are you a virgin?"

I wait for her eyes to go wide as usual when I ask her a personal question, but they don't. It's as if she's exhausted from trying to hide herself from me.

About fucking time.

"No, Sir."

"How many guys have you let in between your sexy legs, little lamb?"

"One, Sir," I wasn't expecting her list of sexual partners to be long, but hearing that she's only been with one other person is a relief. However, her answer is laced with contempt and I want to know why, but now's not the time for that.

"Did he make you feel good? Was he able to make you orgasm?"

This one she doesn't answer. Instead, she looks away as if she's ashamed of something.

"Eyes on me," I command.

She brings her eyes back to mine and I shoot her a look that lets her know I am waiting for an answer.

"No, Sir."

If her last response was laced with contempt, this one is laced with arsenic. Another red-flag on this guy; I'm going to destroy him. I move on quickly, so she doesn't dwell on that last question.

"Have you ever touched yourself before,

like you wanted to do a moment ago?"

"Yes, Sir."

I can see her squeeze her legs together slightly. She's beginning to get turned on again.

"Have you ever given yourself an orgasm?

"No, Sir."

"You've *never* had an orgasm?"

"No! Sir."

"There is nothing wrong with that, don't take my question negatively. Trust me, it's a *huge* turn on knowing that no other random fuckboy has achieved what I'll be able to."

She blushes at my promise.

And it is *a promise, little lamb. I'm going to make you come so hard you're not going to know which way is up.*

"You said you liked how Master Luca took Paige over his knee and spanked her. You liked how he made her moan with pleasure. You're thinking about it, picturing it happening all over again, aren't you?

"Yes, Sir."

"Do you still want to touch yourself?"

"Yes and no, Sir."

"Explain it for me. Tell me what you're

thinking," I request.

Her lips part as she tries to speak, but she's unable to get the words out.

"Don't be embarrassed," I reassure her.

She takes a deep breath.

"Yes, I want to touch myself, but I don't want to touch myself in front of you," she says. "Yet, but possibly one day. Sir."

She is fighting with herself to keep from looking away from me after letting such an intimate part of her show.

"I'm so proud of you, Rosabelle. Thank you for telling me that."

She flashes the smallest sliver of a genuine smile and I'm taking it as a huge win. It's the first time I've seen her without a worried expression or scared scowl on her face.

"I'm not going to make you touch yourself in front of me and I am not going to touch you until you're ready, but there is a third option that I think you'll go for."

She appraises me with skepticism before finally responding.

"Am I allowed to know what it is or am I going in blind?"

"Go into this blindly, and trust that I'll catch you when you fall."

CHAPTER THIRTEEN
Rosabelle

ISWALLOW MY NERVES LIKE I'VE DONE NEARLY every moment of this provocative and exhausting day so far, and its only just past noon.

"I'm not sure about anything, anymore. I don't even know who I am, right now. All I know is that I am tired of making the wrong decisions. Tomorrow, I may feel differently about my choices being taken away from me. But today, the erotic feeling that is swirling around inside of me, wreaking havoc on my body is my driving force. Outside of that, I don't have enough energy to care about anything else."

Who is this person inside of my head making me speak these terrifying words? I feel like I am having an out of body experience and I don't know whether or not I should fight my way back in, or pop some popcorn and see how this all plays out.

I look at The Beast who seems to be desperately trying to prove to me that he is more than what his nickname implies.

"You'll hold your feelings in higher regard by the time I'm finished with you. You'll see exactly how exhilarating it is to leave your fate in the hands of the person entrusted with your care."

His promise comes across as a threat, yet it stokes the fire that is still burning bright within me.

"Yes, Sir."

"Walk to the door and wait for me. I need to go talk to Master Luca for a second and I'll be right there."

I stand in response to his instruction and my conscience screams at me to wake up and realize what is happening. But I've already checked out of reality for the day. At some point between the time that I woke up this morning and now, I managed to lose my Goddamn mind.

The Beast leads me through La Tour and down into the dungeons where I stayed last night. Returning to the place where I woke up this morning makes me shiver, but The Beast assured me that this time my stay would be much more enjoyable than the last.

When we stop walking, we're in the middle of a stone corridor underneath La Tour. I stare at him questioningly, when he places an old, gold skeleton key into a random hole in the middle of the stone wall.

I begin to think that he might be crazy when I hear a loud click as the lock disengages and the hidden door swings open, letting us into a secret, darkened room. Fear begins to overpower me and I find myself moving closer to his side for protection.

What if he is the one that I need protecting from?

"I'm going to have you sit… here," he says, placing his hands on my hips and directing me to sit on a stone chair across the room from where we just entered.

"Stay put, I'll be right back."

"Wait! No!"

A second later I gasp when flames shoot from sconces on the wall, situated at regular intervals around the room. Light floods the space and shines brightly over the seductive scene laid out in front of me.

"This is my personal dungeon," The Beast says, leaning against the wall on the other side of the room.

At first glance, the size of the room takes me by surprise. It looks much too large to fit within the belly of an underground tunnel system. The walls are draped in royal blue velvet with a gold trim. There is a gigantic, beautiful stone fireplace built into one of the walls, with flames roaring inside. Above the fireplace, hangs an intricately carved piece of wood that serves as the mantelpiece. On it, is a gorgeous candelabra and one of the most unique pendulum clocks that I've ever seen. I take a step toward it but stop myself. I look to The Beast for approval. I don't know if I am allowed to move and whether or not there is anything I can and can't touch.

"Feel free to roam. If you find something

that interests you, let me know."

I respond with a small, but genuine smile. As I begin my self-guided tour of the room, I think back to, *holy shit*, was it really only two nights ago that I was here searching for Father? Two nights since I had my first taste of the alluring power of The Beast?

It was a little over 24 hours ago when I swore I would never be a participant in any of the activities within La Tour. I think I am beginning to crack, as laughter tears through my body.

"What is it?" The Beast asks, curious why I'm suddenly laughing in such a serious moment.

I do my best to control my laughter. It takes a moment before I am able to speak.

"I was just thinking back to yesterday morning. It feels like it was lightyears from this moment that I was sitting at my kitchen table thinking about when we met the night before and how terrified I was of you. I'll admit, I was intrigued by the club at the time, but after our tête-à-tête, I swore it was nothing that I would ever be a part of. And now look at me, I am quite literally locked in The Beast's lair."

The reflection of the flames surrounding us

flashes in his dark eyes. It sends a shiver down my spine, but it's different than the frightening chills I felt during our first meeting.

"It's funny how life works out isn't it?" I ask.

"I'm not sure funny is how I would describe it," he says.

I turn and face him, wondering what he means by that. I stare at him waiting for him to elaborate, but he doesn't. I don't ask him. First, because I don't know if that's allowed but second because even if it is, I don't think he would answer me anyway. Everyone has dark secrets; I wonder what his are.

Before I can get too wrapped up in thought I hear him speak again.

"Are you still wet, little lamb?"

My cheeks flush at his words.

"If not, I have just the thing to get you worked up again."

"I am still a little wet," I say, shyly, "but I'm not quite as turned on as I was upstairs."

"I'd like to try something. Do you trust me?"

"I trust you," I tell him, realizing that, though it's crazy, it's true.

"Good girl," he says.

He places his hand on the small of my back and directs me to an odd-looking piece of furniture in the corner of the room. It looks like one of those pommel horses that the men's gymnastics team flips over in their event. Do you know what this is, little lamb?"

"No, Sir."

"It's called a spanking bench. While I believe that you would enjoy being spanked very much, I promised that I wasn't going to touch you today, and as you know I always keep my promises. But I would still like to bind you to it, and introduce you to the flogger this evening."

I swallow nervously.

"Do you know what a flogger is, little lamb?"

"I think so."

"Have you ever had one used on you before?"

"No, Sir."

"Don't be intimidated by it. Sometimes it's used for pain, but mostly it's for pleasure. Once you're further along in your training, I think you'll find that you will enjoy the flogger for both."

Walking to a set of hooks on the wall nearby, he picks up the item that he had in his hand in the dream I had yesterday.

"Tell me what you're thinking."

"I'm nervous. I didn't believe that spanking could feel good but my mind changed upon seeing Paige enjoy it as much as she did."

"Good, Rosabelle. Remove your skirt. I want you to kneel on the edge of the bench and lay your body over the hump. I'm going to restrain you to it with your ass high in the air. Once you are in position, I'll explain what's going to happen next."

I do as he says and climb up onto the bench. I can already feel my nerve endings heightening in anticipation of what is to come. The way my body reacted to watching Paige getting her ass spanked in the training room was intoxicating and addicting, and I'm really looking forward to feeling that way again. Without a second thought, I lean over and place my elbows on the other side of the bench. Sticking my ass high in the air for him already has my clit throbbing, again.

Is he going to make me come like this? I hope so.

He was right, it was only a matter of time before I begged him for it.

"You're absolutely breathtaking, little lamb," he says.

My pussy clenches at his words.

"I'm going to start off slow. I will add more power based on your reaction. If at any time you feel uncomfortable or something hurts and you need me to stop, say 'red'. If you're uncomfortable with something and you need me to ease up, say 'yellow'. Understood?"

"Yes, Sir."

"Good."

The first hit doesn't hurt at all. The suede tails are soft and they tickle my skin as The Beast whips the flogger through the air. He hits me with the tails over and over again, softly and it almost feels like a massage. It's relaxing. Between that and the erotic position that I am in, it doesn't take any time at all for the moisture to build up again.

I am enjoying the feel of it, when suddenly The Beast increases the power behind his hit, taking me by surprise. I expect the slight sting to interfere negatively, but it has the opposite effect and the increased pleasure elicits a moan from me.

"My little lamb is enjoying herself."

"Yes, Sir," I pant.

He swings the flogger down on my ass several more times, each with equal power, and I cry out.

"Oh my, God!"

"Does that hurt?"

"No, Sir."

"Tell me, little lamb," he says, bringing his face close to mine. "If I were to remove your panties, would they be a little wet or would they be soaking?"

His words make me pant.

"Yes, Sir."

"A little wet, Sir."

He swings the flogger several more times with the same exhilarating effect that it had before and I cry out again.

"I think my little lamb is ready to come, am I right?"

"Yes, Sir."

My stomach drops when he begins to untie

me. I whine in response thinking that he's going to work me up and make me stay that way.

"Don't worry, little lamb. I'm not done with you."

What else does he have planned? Just as I am about to break down and beg him to touch me, exactly like he said I would, he answers my silent question.

He helps me down from the bench and points to a chair across from it.

"Remove your skirt and sit there."

I pull my skirt down my legs and leave it lying where it falls on the floor beneath me. When I sit down, he cuffs my legs to the chair before tying my hands together behind the back of the chair. He walks to another part of the room and returns with a vibrating wand in his hand. My eyes go wide when I see it.

"I'm keeping my promise of not touching you, don't worry," he laughs. "Have you ever used one of these before?"

"No, Sir."

"Oh, this is going to be fun," he says with an evil smile on his face.

He presses a button on the side of the wand

and it buzzes to life.

"Let's turn the speed up," he says, pressing the button two more times. "No need to drag this out any further. It's time to put my little lamb out of her misery. In the future, you'll be required to ask before you're allowed to come, but today you can come whenever you're ready, okay?"

I nod my head. I'm having a hard time keeping my wits about me at the moment.

"You say "Yes, Sir" or I'm going to leave you tied to the chair and unsatisfied for the rest of the day."

"Yes, Sir. I'm sorry, Sir."

His gaze turns serious as he lowers the wand and places it against my core, over my panties. Instantly, my eyes roll back into my head as heat licks up my torso. A loud moan escapes from my mouth and my hips begin rocking back and forth on the chair. Each movement rocks my clit against the head of the wand sending another zing of pleasure buzzing through me.

"That's it, move your hips," The Beast encourages me.

I never knew this kind of pleasure existed.

At this moment, in the middle of this lewd, messed up, fucking exciting situation, I'm glad I've never been able to orgasm before. To have this be my first experience is utter bliss.

A new feeling builds deep within me and rises up quickly. My moans turn into screams of pleasure as the euphoria that hits me is insurmountable. It spreads over my whole body like a wave crashing down on the shore. The feeling is addicting and I never want it to end.

It's over all too soon and when The Beast removes the vibrator from in between my legs, I feel like I could cry, I already miss the feel of it so much.

"How was that, little lamb?"

"Incredible, Sir. Thank you," I gasp, barely able to catch my breath.

He removes the cuffs from my legs and unties my hands. "Can you stand?"

"I think so," I say, giving it a try.

When I'm up, I place my hand on the back of the chair to help hold me steady.

"How do you feel?"

I look down, ashamed.

"Rosabelle, look at me," he commands.

I look him in the eye again.

"How do you feel? As your Dom, it's my responsibility to make sure that you're okay."

"I feel bad."

"What do you mean?"

"I mean, you just gave me this incredible orgasm and all I can think about is having another one as quickly as possible."

"Don't ever feel bad about that. Women can have many, many orgasms. We'll have to try that one day," he smiles, evilly. "Rosabelle, do you need to come again?"

"Yes, Sir," I say, as a tear falls down my face.

"Don't cry, little lamb. Tell me what you'd like to try next."

He waves his hand at the room and my eyes fall on the one piece of furniture that I actually recognize.

"I... think I need another person's touch, Sir."

He follows my gaze to the bed.

"You knew I would beg you for it. This is me, *begging you*, to touch me, Sir."

I don't know what I anticipated would happen when I finally said the words, but the last thing I thought this *evil beast* would do would be to sweep me into his arms, carry me to the bed, and make love to me like he never wants to lose me.

CHAPTER FOURTEEN
The Beast

THE HOOPS THAT I AM NEEDING TO GO THROUGH just to get my own fucking money back is ridiculous. I'm reading through an email from the bank where Reggie was sending the money he was siphoning off me. Mayhew was able to discover the account number and from there we located the bank, which is in the middle of the Caribbean.

I hit forward and send the email to Mayhew because, fuck if I know what any of this financial stuff means. There was a reason I hired Reggie in the first place, God damn it!

My concentration is broken by a very light knock on my door.

"What?" I shout, annoyed.

"I'm sorry, I'll come back," I hear the sweet voice of my little lamb and I finally look up from my computer.

"Rosabelle!" I call after her and she stops, turning back toward my office.

"Come in," I say.

She smiles shyly and I wonder why she's still so nervous around me. I'll have to ask her the next time we're in a session.

"Have a seat," I command her.

She waited by the door for my instruction like she's supposed to and it makes me so proud. She looks absolutely ravishing, as she does every day, and I can't wait until I can be with her again. It's been a few days since I made love to her in my dungeon. I had no intention of taking her so soon, but I don't regret a moment of what we shared.

"How are you today?"

"Fine, Sir. How are you?"

"Better now that you're here."

Her face lights up with delight at my compliment.

"What brings you here?"

She leans forward and places a piece of

paper on my desk.

"I wrote a letter to my father. I thought that you should read it, and if you approve, I will send it to him."

When I look up at her, she's already looking down at her hands in her lap. I pick up the letter from my desk and read it.

Dear Father,

I'm writing to tell you that I am doing well and enjoying my new life at Le Château, so there is no cause for you to worry.

In the short amount of time that I've been here, I've come to realize that I was living a very disparaging life for the past three years. I wasn't being fair to myself. I am a young woman and I should have been going to school and making friends, rather than forced to work 60 hours a week to take care of a father who emotionally abandoned me at a time when I needed him the most.

You're weren't the only one who lost someone when Mother passed away. It was an incredibly unfair thing you did to me, Father. I would like to think that I can forgive you for it one day, but I won't even consider it until you're a sober, responsible, contributing member of society like you used to be.

Should that day ever come, you're welcome to make an attempt to prove it to me. Only then will I consider letting you be part of my life again. I will always love you, but I can't allow you to disrespect me and hold me back any longer.

Love,
Rosabelle

"I can't imagine that it was easy for you to write this, little lamb."

I wish that I would have had the balls to tell my parents how I felt about them before they died.

"No, Sir."

"Are you sure that you want to send this?"

"Yes, Sir."

I pick up my phone and call Dex.

"Hey man, can you come to my office and grab something to put in the mail? Thanks."

I hang up the phone and search for an envelope and a stamp. When I find them, I place everything on the desk in front of her so she can stuff and address the envelope.

"I'm really proud of you, I want you to know that. This is a huge deal and I love that you thought to do it."

"Thank you, Sir."

"How would you like to do something special today? Just you and me?"

"Like what, Sir?"

"Whatever *you* want. I want to show you how proud I am of my little lamb."

Again, her face lights up with excitement and I fucking love how happy she is.

"Can we go for a walk in the rose garden?"

"If that's what you want to do, then that's what we'll do."

I look at my watch, it's 11:15.

"Give me 45 minutes and I will meet you in your room."

"Yes, Sir. Thank you!"

"It's so beautiful out here," Rosabelle says, once we enter the garden.

"Have you gotten a chance to walk through it yet?"

"No, Sir."

"I have to admit that I don't come out here often enough."

"Roses are my favorite flower," she says.

I notice her lift her right hand and as she inspects it, a sad look falls across her face. I still have her ring. I haven't had the chance to give it back to her, yet.

"Do you like roses because of your name or…?

"Roses were my mother's favorite flower. That's how I got my name."

"What happened to her?"

"She got sick and passed away three years ago."

"I'm sorry to hear that, Rosabelle," I say, heartbroken for her.

"Thank you, Sir."

We walk in silence for a few moments before she speaks again.

"May I ask you a question, Sir?"

"Sure."

"Do you have any family?"

She had to ask that one, huh?

I decide to answer her question. "No, I'm an

only child and my parents died 10 years ago."

"I'm so sorry. I'm sorry to bring it up."

"It's okay, you didn't know. It was a long time ago."

I take her by the hand and place a kiss on the back of it.

"Let's keep walking, I have a surprise up here for you."

Her eyes go wide like they always do when she's nervous and I squeeze her hand gently to reassure her. We walk the rest of this row and turn left, then down the next row, then we make a right to put us in the dead center of the middle of the garden. When we get there, the picnic lunch that I had the kitchen staff put together is already waiting for us.

"Here we go, have a seat on the blanket and I'll see what the chef prepared for us. Cheese, fruit, crackers, chicken, and wine."

I call out the names of everything as I take them out of the basket. I grab the corkscrew and open the bottle of Pinot Grigio.

"Do you like wine?"

"I've never really been much of a drinker," she replies.

"I'll pour you a small glass, I'm sure you'll like it."

"Thank you, Sir."

I check the basket to make sure that I didn't miss anything.

"And that's it," I confirm.

Rosabelle giggles and it puts a smile on my face.

"Listen to you, giggling over there. What's so funny?"

"Nothing, Sir. It's silly," she answers and waves her hand, like that will actually make me drop it.

"Rosabelle. I asked you what you're giggling about," I use my stern voice to draw it out of her, even though I'm not really angry.

I immediately regret it because her gorgeous smile diminishes quickly.

"I'm sorry, Sir. I was just thinking that I was surprised when you didn't pull a toy out of the basket. You always seem to have something handy whenever we're together."

This time I let out a small laugh to try and lighten the mood back up.

"You know, you can use anything as a toy, it

doesn't have to be something made specifically as a sexual implement."

My eyes narrow slyly and I'm happy to see that she doesn't appear as nervous as she usually does.

"Shall I show you?"

I know her answer before she says it, evidenced by the deep red blush heating her cheeks right now.

"Rosabelle, I love how responsive you are and I look forward to your reaction every time I'm near."

Her cheeks light up even brighter. I stand up and hold my hand out to help her.

"Strip out of your clothes and lie down on the blanket,"

"Out here?" I glare at her and she changes her reaction. "I'm sorry! Yes, Sir!"

"I promise, no one will be able to see you."

"Yes, Sir."

I walk to one of the bushes and pick a rose that has a large bloom on it. When I turn around, my eyes land on my little lamb looking good enough to eat on the blanket. *I think I just might...*

"Good girl," I say to her.

I reach into the basket and pull out the wine tool, which has a small knife on it used for cutting the foil on a wine bottle. I use it to cut the thorns from the stem of the flower so I don't accidentally scrape Rosabelle's skin.

"Close your eyes for me and relax. Nothing I do is going to be painful, okay?

"Yes, Sir," she says, eyes already closed.

I take a moment to appreciate her body before getting started. She is gorgeous. Her nipples are tight little peaks from the light breeze, and I can already see a slight glistening near the opening of her pussy. The sight of her like this drives me wild. My cock thickens with my building hunger and I know that I will be tasting her today.

I place the bud of the rose on her chest, between her tits, before circling each of them a few times. I run the bud down her stomach in small circular motions, getting close to her pussy, and then backing away again. I see her fists tighten a few times in response and hear the moan escape from her throat.

The next time I drag the flower down her

stomach, I veer to the right and continue the soft, circular motions down her right leg. When I get to her foot, I remove the flower and lightly tickle the bottom of her foot. Her leg jumps and it makes me smile. Then, I drag the flower back up her leg. I run it dangerously close to her pussy, but don't touch it, yet. Instead, I drag the flower down her left leg, repeating what I did with the right.

When I get back to the center between her legs, I run the flower around her pussy a few times before I run it down her closed slit.

I hear another moan of pleasure.

"Open your legs for me, Rosabelle."

She opens her legs, but not far enough.

"Wider."

She spreads them as wide as she can go, completely opening herself up to me. I can see her bright red pussy, glistening with her juices that have escaped from deep inside.

"Beautiful."

I touch the bud of the rose to her clit and I rub the area in circles, eliciting a louder moan from her this time. Then, I smack her on her clit with it a few times. I run it up right up the middle of her pussy, collecting some of her moisture on the petals before I bring it to my nose and inhale deeply.

"Intoxicating."

I place the rose down on the blanket and grab the bottle of wine.

"Whatever you do, Rosabelle, stay as still as possible, understood?"

"Yes, Sir."

I take a sip of wine from the bottle and hold my mouth over her pussy. I let some of it slither from my lips and she gasps in surprise the moment the cold liquid hits her hot core. When she's settled again, I let more liquid through and receive another gasp, but this time it's accompanied by a moan.

I take another sip of wine, but this time put my mouth directly over her clit, so close that it's almost touching her. I open my mouth and let it spill out all over her pussy. When her body jumps, I close my lips around her clit and suck on it. She cries out in surprise and pleasure.

I take her tiny hips in my hands and hold her down so she can't wiggle around. I suck on her clit until she starts begging to come and then I release her, and stick my tongue inside of her, then I move back up to her clit and suck again. But this time when she begs to come, I tell her to do it.

She squirts all over the place, making a mess. I catch some in my mouth and drink it all up. The taste of her is just as intoxicating as the rest of her is. When her orgasm subsides, I crawl up her body and place my lips over hers. She opens up and lets my tongue in.

Eventually, I break the kiss and stand, telling her to stay put, as I quickly undress. Once I've shed all of my clothing, I move over the top of her and grab my cock. Running the head through her soaking wet slit, I line it up with her pussy and push my way in. She cries out with pleasure and pulls her legs up, allowing me to sink deeper inside of her. It only takes a few minutes before she's coming again.

"That's it, little lamb, come all over my cock," I tell her.

As if my encouragement spurred her on, she comes again. I thrust harder mid-orgasm, drawing it out for her until she screams. Her pussy clenches around me so tightly that I come seconds later.

"God! *Fuck*! Rosabelle, you're so fucking amazing."

I place my forehead on her chest between her tits, needing a place to rest it while I catch my breath.

"I love everything about you," I say against her chest.

I wait for her to say something, but she doesn't. When I look up again, I see that her hand is over her eyes and she looks like she's crying.

"Fuck! Rosabelle, what's wrong?"

I climb off her and sit down, picking her up and pulling her onto my lap. She drops her head into her hands and continues crying.

"Rosabelle, I need to know what's wrong. Now. Did I hurt you?"

"N--no!" she manages to get out in between sobs.

"What then? Baby, talk to me."

"I don't know! I'm so confused!"

"About what?"

"About how I feel. I've never felt so happy. I love spending time with you, but I barely know you! I'm worried that the more you get to know me, the less you will like, and you'll eventually tire of me.

"Rosabelle, look at me."

She lifts her face up out of her hands and I can finally see her gorgeous hazel eyes.

"First, I will *never* get tired of you.

"But how do you know that? We've only just met."

"Rosabelle, from the moment my eyes landed on you in La Tour I knew that you were special. I had to get to you and find out who you were. I scared you away that night because I was afraid. I didn't want to be drawn to you.

"But why?"

"My ex-died a few years ago. I haven't wanted to be with anyone since then, until you. Then, when Dex and the guys brought you into the dungeon, I knew it was fate. That you were meant to be in my life. I didn't want to believe it, but I knew it was true. I know this is scary, but we're in it together. I'm not letting you go; I was serious when I said that. You're mine, Rosabelle, forever."

I lean down and kiss her again, happy when

she places her hand on my cheek and kisses me back. After several seconds, I pull away from her and look into her eyes.

"Are you okay?" I ask.

"I'm okay, Sir," she pauses, considering her next words, "but I don't think that I will ever look at roses the same way again."

She starts giggling through her tears and the sound is like music to my ears.

"Let's get eating, you're probably hungry. I know I am," I tell her.

"Well, I do have an appetite, but it's not for food," she says to me.

I look up at her and she crawls back onto my lap with a seductive and hungry look on her face.

My sexy, little lamb.

CHAPTER FIFTEEN
Rosabelle

THE PAST TWO WEEKS HAVE BEEN UNLIKE anything that I would have ever imagined for myself. I've had training sessions every day and Master B and I have been working, strenuously, on our new relationship. We're getting to know one another and finding some middle ground. While it hasn't been easy, it's opened my eyes to an entirely different way of life, submission aside.

He's given me confidence that I never thought was possible. I truly feel strong, beautiful, and respected. I'm not second-guessing every decision that I make any longer and for the first time in my life, I am able to focus on myself.

Despite the progress I've been making, I managed to get myself into trouble two nights ago, and I think Master B may still be upset with me. He had planned for us to have dinner in his private quarters that evening and told me to be ready at exactly 7:00. He wanted to do something special for me since I've been working so hard.

I had a little bit of free time until then and decided to explore my new home. I found the kitchen, a gym, and the most extraordinary library that I've ever seen. It pulled me in and I spent a while looking through all of the books deciding to take one outside to read in the garden.

It was there, at 8:15 that a furious Master B found me. He tore me from the chaise where I was seated and bent me over the side of it. Lifting my skirt, I received a painful, unforgiving spanking.

I began crying and pleading with him to let me explain that I had simply lost track of time. When he had finished spanking me outside, he dragged me through Le Château and down to his dungeon. The harder I cried, the longer the punishment became.

He secured me to the bondage bench and brought me close to orgasm over and over again with his fingers deep inside of me as he held the vibrating wand to my clit.

Each time I was mere seconds away from bliss, he would remove his fingers and turn off the wand, causing my orgasm to fade away and leaving me unfulfilled and wanting more. It was sheer torture and it went on for hours, not ending until I was teetering on the edge, achingly close to euphoria but unable to reach it. Then, he placed a chastity belt on me so I wouldn't be able to touch myself and sent me to bed alone.

I thrashed around all night, in more pain from the need for release than from the spanking that I'd received. My entire body felt as if it was on fire, and I began screaming in discomfort, knowing it wouldn't do anything.

When Master B found me rocking back and forth in the corner of my room the next morning, he removed the belt and carried me to my bed. I sobbed like I haven't done since I was a baby and told him how sorry I was. He told me to lie back and he flicked my clit and finger-fucked my pussy until stars exploded in my vision and I passed out from the intense pleasure.

When I awoke, he was still in bed with me, his large body curled around mine from behind. When I turned to him to see whether or not he was awake, our eyes locked and he leaned down, placing his lips on mine gently.

It wasn't the first time that we kissed, but it was the first time that it was laced with more than possession and desire. There was no mistaking the love that I felt in it.

I've just finished getting ready for the evening when I look at my reflection in the mirror and watch my cheeks go flush with need thinking about that night.

"What are you thinking about?"

As if the mere thought of him caused him to appear, Master B breaks through my trance and I look from myself to him, standing behind me in the doorway to the bathroom.

I turn to face him.

"I was thinking about when you punished me the other night."

"Were you?" he asks with a surprised tone.

"Yes, Sir."

"Were you remembering how it made you feel? Now you know what will happen if you ever defy me again, little lamb."

"Yes, Sir," I begin. "It was horrible while it was happening, but thinking back to it..." I have to take a deep breath.

He closes the distance between us and my skin burns hotter the nearer he gets. He places his palm tenderly on my cheek, spurring me on.

"Yes, Rosabelle?"

"Not that I would dream of defying you, causing myself to be tortured so thoroughly again, but I was thinking that I wouldn't mind experiencing a less intense version of that."

The air around us thickens with desire. He places his strong arms around me, and gently grabs a fistful of my hair, tilting my head back for me to look at him.

"You're making it difficult for me to not call off the special night that I have planned so I can take you down to the dungeon right now and fulfill every one of your wishes, little lamb."

A grateful smile blooms on my face and he leans in for a kiss.

"I'm all ready for our night. I just finished,"

I say when he pulls away again.

"Good. Come, I have something to give you."

He takes me by the hand and leads me to the tufted bench at the end of my bed, and pulls me down onto his lap.

"I took this the first night you were here. I noticed that it could use a little touching-up," he says, withdrawing something from his pocket.

He flips his hand over showing me what's in his palm.

"My mother's ring!" My eyes well up with tears.

I can't believe that I'd forgotten about it.

"I had my jeweler buff the band and clean it up. I also noticed that it was about a quarter of a size too big, so I had him resize it."

"I thought it was gone forever."

"I'm sorry to have made you think that you lost it, but I wanted to surprise you," he explains.

"It's okay, I'm just so happy to have it back! Thank you for restoring its original beauty."

I throw my arms around him and press my lips against his. It's the first time that I've ever initiated contact with Master B., and I pull away, afraid that I've broken a rule. When he places his hands on my cheeks and pulls me back to him, he kisses me as if he will never be able to get his fill.

"Rosabelle," he says, breaking the kiss.

"I'm sorry!" I say, thinking I've upset him somehow.

"There is nothing to be sorry for, but we have to stop. If not, we are going to miss our special night for the second time this week. Starting with this."

He stands and walks to my dresser, returning with a wide, flat, black velvet box.

"I have something to ask you," he says, sitting down and opening the box.

Inside is a stunning, delicate gold chain with a ruby- and diamond-studded rose pendant attached to it.

I take in the beauty of the necklace as Master B speaks again

"This necklace represents my vow to you, Rosabelle. My vow to take responsibility for you and always make sure that you feel loved and cherished. I will always praise you, believe in you, and encourage you. I will be aware of your needs and ensure they're met. I will punish you only when it's appropriate and promise never to use more force than necessary. This will strengthen our bond and the life that we share will never falter."

What he's said is unexpected and somewhat overwhelming, but he's just putting into words everything that he's been doing for me since the moment that I opened my mind and set myself free.

"Rosabelle, are you ready to be mine, forever?"

At one time in my life I would have considered it crazy, but being here has changed everything I ever knew. I wanted adventure and now, here with My Beast, I've finally gotten what I wished for.

"Yes, Sir."

*** KEEP A LOOKOUT FOR MORE TALES FROM LA TOUR ***

Never Lost

Shadows are formed by objects blocking rays of light.

Just not mine.

Its darkness is ever-present, taunting me, tricking me into doing things a man should never do, but I've learned to embrace it.

Will she?

Lost in dreams of a life anywhere but here, she's ignorant to the danger perched just outside the window.

Taking her will be easy.

But can I teach her to fly?

Prologue

H IS FACE IS PLASTERED OVER EVERY TABLOID in the checkout line. A mix of both; professionally posed images, on the more reputable magazines, and shots taken from a considerable distance on the lesser-known rags. Each with its own version of what is going on in the life of yet another A-list celebrity.

Now the Most Eligible Bachelor in Hollywood.

Emotional Breakup for Our Beloved Preston.

Tinka Caught Kissing A Life Lost in Neverland Producer.

Preston and Tinka were once America's favorite on and off-screen couple. Cast in more than ten movies together they raked in millions, but as with many famous pairings, it ended almost as quickly as it started. The details of what happened between them is still somewhat of a mystery. Unreliable sources say infidelity played a part, while others say it was a mutual separation.

Whatever the reason, it hasn't hurt Preston's career. He's booked for three movies over the next five years and two new TV series that, if the pilots do well, will put him in a long-term contract.

Tinka, on the other hand, hasn't had it as easy. Against her agent's wishes, she began dating publicly before the breakup was officially announced. It put her in a negative light with everyone in the industry, except one—the paparazzi. They've had a field day snapping her picture every chance they get and in the most unflattering ways. With only one movie contract in the past year, her lavish style of living is at risk.

It's a sad tale of what could have been.

Faithful fans were devastated, posting crying GIFs and offering their sympathies on social media, all the while never giving up hope of a reconciliation. But not everyone felt the same. Some rallied around the idea of a breakup, because if Preston is single, there's the smallest chance they could have a turn with the king of the big screen.

I can't blame them, with his dark hair, dark eyes, and a body chiseled from the side of a mountain, Preston Pace is a decadent god.

ACKNOWLEDGEMENTS
Thank you

Ally Vance – Thank you for going through this story with a fine-tooth comb. You helped shape it to the beauty that it is today!

My Beta Readers –Ashley Allen, Ashley Cestra, Kirsty Adams, and Patty Walker – A big thank you for all of your help, always! (Especially for all of the last-minute reads!!!)

My Street Team – For always working your asses off to get my name out there. My notifications are constantly blowing up because of you and each and every one of them brings a smile to my face and tears to my eyes. Knowing how much you all support me means everything in the world! You're the best!

To my family – thank you always for your love and support. I wouldn't be able to do what I do without you.

ABOUT

Murphy Wallace is an International Bestselling Author with works in several different genres, but most of her work as been in Dark Romantic Suspense. She currently resides in a small Eastern Florida town with her husband, who doubles as her best friend and their two boys.

When she's not getting in touch with her inner child at Disney World, or enjoying everything that Florida has to offer with her family, she enjoys writing and watching true crime documentaries.

She has a cat named Maisy who is her constant writing partner.

FIND MURPHY

Online

Profile: http://bit.ly/MurphyWallace
Page: http://bit.ly/AuthorMurphyWallace
Group: http://bit.ly/MurphysLovers
BookBub: http://bit.ly/MurphyBB
Instagram: http://bit.ly/InstaMurph
Twitter: http://bit.ly/MurphyTwitter
Goodreads: http://bit.ly/MWGoodreads
Email: authormurphywallace@gmail.com

ALSO BY
Murphy

The Wildheart Duet
Stolen Love
With Love

Inferno World
Obloquy

Cavalieri Della Morte
Sorrow's Queen
Co-written with Ashleigh Giannoccaro

Coming Soon
K. Bromberg's Driven World
Octane

Printed in Great Britain
by Amazon